Unrequited Love

and

Other Short Stories

by

Carl Crozier

Unrequited Love and Other Short Stories

Carl Crozier

ISBN-10: 0-9977051-5-9
ISBN-13: 978-0-9977051-5-7

Library of Congress Control Number: 2017917338

This novel is a work of fiction. Names, characters, businesses, places, events and incidents are the products of the author's imagination or used fictitiously. Any resemblance to actual persons, living or dead, businesses, companies, events or locales is coincidental.

Printed in the United States of America.

BELLA JOHNS ENTERPRISES
PUBLISHER

CONTENTS

INTRODUCTION

I am sure that many fictional stories are based upon situations that are indeed partially factual. A number of people have had incidents that have happened in their lives that could be material for a novel are at least a short story when put in the hands of a writer with a vivid imagination. All that needs to be done is to take the facts of the incident that happened, investigate the details and then put a fictional piece to the beginning, middle part or the ending of the occurrence to create the story. You then have what I call a true/fictionalized story.

A good occurrence in someone's life can be recorded and then a narrative can be developed to create an interesting work of fiction.

Example: (Fact) John won the lottery. (Fiction) He met and married a nurse who recognized that John was wealthy. She courted and married him for his money. John ended his life after the nurse spent his money and left him for broke. The above was a **good true** happening event that was turned into a fictionalized **bad** ending event. A story can also have a bad event that is turned into a fictionalized good event.

The following stories are all based upon true incidents that happened in the lives of the charters in the story. It's up to the readers of the stories to discern which parts of the stories are true and which parts are fictionalized.

Have fun analyzing.

UNREQUITED LOVE

Wake up and get out of bed at 5:30 AM. Brush your teeth, take a shower, comb your hair and dress. Cook some breakfast, eat it, drink a cup of coffee, put the finishing touch to your grooming and you are out the door - heading for work. Slide into your car, Start the engine and you roar out of your driveway on to the pavement in front of your residence. You have to travel 10 blocks on your route before you reach the main highway which leads to your job. All of a sudden you see this vehicle, an SUV, coming at you at a high rate of speed. It's swerving, side to side, as it approaches you on the narrow street that you are traveling. Behind the vehicle, that is coming toward you, you see flashing blue lights. You try to react to the approaching careening SUV by turning the steering wheel in the opposite direction of that of the approaching vehicle. The narrow street, with cars parked on both sides, doesn't give you or the approaching vehicle much room to maneuver. You slam on your breaks hoping that the vehicle will have room to pass on your left side. It does not have room to pass. The vehicle slams into your car, head on. Your car is smashed and so is your body. In an instant you are dead. A life is taken in an instant because the police were chasing a teenager in a stolen car.

Life can end in an instant and for some humans it does. Many (maybe most) of us live to reach an age wherein we naturally die. There are many exceptions. Beside accidents, you can be murdered, die in a natural disaster, breathe your last breath in a war related incident or your life can be taken away early in a health-related demise.

Sharon Wentworth can attest to life being ended in an instant (well almost) because of health reasons. Sharon, a 53-year-old career Black woman gets out of bed one fateful morning and begins the regiment of getting ready for work.   She showers and returns to her bedside to get dressed where she has laid out the days apparel. Sharon does not remember this but all of a sudden, she experiences dizziness, her vision becomes blurred, she loses her balance and falls to the floor. Her brain loses function and she passes out. Blood flow to her brain has been cut off. Sharon has had a stroke. A stroke is a brain attack as opposed to a heart attack. Because of her brain cells being deprived of oxygen and the needed glucose, the blood flow to her brain has been cut off. Sharon loses consciousness. She lies naked on her bedroom floor. She lives in her house alone. No one is there to witness the medical dilemma that she has just experienced. Unless she receives medical attention, Sharon will die.

Sharon works for a Title Insurance Company and she occupies a prestigious position within the company. She is a closer. A closer ensures that when a property is sold the records are searched in order that the title to the property is free and clear and there are no leans or debts on the property. Documents are viewed and legal representative from both parties negotiate the sale. The closer ensures that the sale is properly executed, and the property is clear for the sale. It is tedious research work which ends when the seller and buyer of the property sit down with the closer to finalize the sale of the property. Sharon has worked for the company for a number of years and is a valued employee. Starting as a clerk, she rose through the ranks to become a closer. On the fateful day of her stroke, Sharon is scheduled to close on two properties. She is a workaholic and never misses work. When she does not show for work her employer calls her house but receives no answer. Sharon had filled out a form required by her employer that indicated who to contact in case of emergency. The employer pulled the form and contacted the first number listed on the form. It was Sharon's next-door neighbor. The neighbor indicated that she had not seen Sharon since last night but as she talked, she saw out of her window that Sharon's car was still in the drive way. The neighbor indicated to the employer that she would ring Sharon's bell. She walked across her lawn to Sharon's house and rang her bell and knocked on the door. When she did not receive an answer, she begin to walk around the property to see if she could spot Sharon in the house. The blinds in Sharon's one story, bedroom window were partially open and the neighbor could see clothes on the bed but she could not see Sharon. As best she could, she looked into the bed room and saw that the light was still on which aroused her suspension. The neighbor had known Sharon for some time and knew her when she was married. She knew that Sharon and her ex-husband, though divorced, were on good terms with each other because the husband had custody of their child, who was almost grown. She had his number and she knew that he had keys to the house. At that point, the neighbor determined that she would call Sharon's ex-husband who lived in the vicinity. The ex-husband was contacted and told that Sharon could not be contacted but her car was still in the driveway. He indicated that he would come over and enter the house as soon as he could get away from a task that he was involved in. An hour later, he arrived at the house and saw the neighbor waiting on her porch for him. Together they entered Sharon's house. Calling Sharon's name, as they went through the house, they proceeded to the bed room where they spotted Sharon laying naked on the bed room floor. They both hurried to Sharon in an effort to arouse her. She had a pulse, but Sharon did not respond to their call or their touch. The ex-husband called 911.

The ambulance with emergency medical technicians arrived within 15 minutes of the call and the technicians began to work on Sharon while they prepared her for transportation to the hospital. Since Sharon was unconscious, the technicians had to assume that she had had either a heart attack or a stroke and they administered special clot clearing medication on the way to the hospital. Sharon arrived at the hospital and was transported to the emergency room where a C.T scan was performed which confirmed that she had suffered a stroke. Sharon was given additional treatment in the ER and then transferred to intensive care. She came to consciousness in intensive care, but it was evident that her cognitive functions were impaired. Over time, through work with the hospital staff in intensive care and the administration of medication, Sharon was able to regain much of her strength and after a period of time she was entered into a rehabilitation program. She gained most of her normal bodily functions that she had prior to the stroke with the exception of memory loss. Sharon had trouble retaining facts and figures that were essential in her job as a Real Estate Closer. Thus, she was unable to go back to work after recovering from the Stroke. Sharon was damaged but the medical problem that she experienced didn't kill her. She lived to carry on her life - though it would be different from what it had been prior to her medical dilemma. Sharon beat death.

Sharon had made a very good living as a result of her work. Her income, plus bonuses that she received had put her in a high-income bracket that allowed her to be financially independent. Upon losing her ability to work, Sharon had savings through her 401K profit sharing program and savings in the bank. She applied for and eventually received Social Security disability payments. The income from those sources allowed her to remain monetarily independent.

Sharon came to Chicago from Georgia when she graduated from high school. She was determined to leave the south and come to Chicago to better her prospects for economic success. She had an aunt in Chicago who invited her to come and stay. Upon coming to Chicago, Sharon applied herself to do the things needed to successfully advance her life. She secured employment in various occupations at low levels of income. Sharon realized that she needed to augment her work experience with some educational expertise to expand her qualifications for better jobs. She foregoes academic education to enroll in a business college in order to concentrate on a business curriculum. Bookkeeping, stenography, marketing and business accounting are subjects that she wants to become proficient in. Sharon matriculates through the business school courses and is awarded with a job with the aforementioned Title Company. She advances from a beginning clerk to a closer position within the company and becomes a truly valuable asset to her employer. She has completed numerous closings and received various awards for her work

By the time of her stroke, Sharon has reached financial success, but she was not successful in her personal life. She has been through two failed marriages and has had failed relationships with numerous mates. A son, was a product of one of her failed marriages. The lady was a beautiful young Black woman. She stands about 5 feet 2 inches, had a light brown skin complexion in her younger days but her skin color darkened as she became older and the stroke might have also been responsible for her change in complexion as an older woman. To say that she was shapely in her younger days was an understatement. Sharon was a male magnet and woman also paid attention and desired her body. Her good looks and her out-going personality were an attraction for both males and females and she dabbled in various erotic situations. She would be the center of attention in any social setting even if she didn't have all of her physical attributes. Though Sharon was attractive and outgoing, she had personality defects. She was self-centered, self-absorbed and selfish. Her needs were always put above the needs of others. She had a disregard for the rights and feelings of those she had relations with. There was a lack of empathy and she was cold and calculating for what she wanted. She had a value system that she did not have trust in others and her value system did not include principles for the emotions of those that she had relations with. She believed that she could not trust others because she had to rely on her judgment alone. Her 'no's' were emphatic when she disagreed with the subject under consideration. There was no room for compromise or negotiations. Her financial success contributed to her assessment of her life decisions. After all, she made the money and did not stand for contrary opinions in her life. It was either her way or get out of her life.

As Sharon grew older, age begin to deduct from the physical attributes that had made her so wanted. She grew fat. Between the age of 18 to 53 she went from a size 8 to a size 16. She still was able to be a social gadfly because fat Black woman are not an oddity in the community. Many Black women put on the poundage as they grow older and it is accepted that weight will accumulate on many a Black woman. But weight can be a killer. Weight was thought to be one of the factors or causes in Sharon's Stroke. The weight gain cost Sharon some of her sex appeal but she still was a good-looking woman and her sex appeal was not entirely lost. she was also eager to socialize - on her own terms. She was successful at making friends but not keeping them because of her controlling personality. After the stroke, when Sharon was in rehab, her main emphasis was to lose weight. She outlined a regiment of diet and exercise that if followed would allow her to shed the excess poundage. Sharon also began to step dance. Stepping is a form of dancing that is very popular in the Black community of Chicago. Stepping is to Black people what salsa is to the Hispanic community.

Since she could no longer work, Sharon main pursuit in life became regaining her health, taking care of her house and recapturing the beauty of her youth to the extent that a 53-year-old woman could do so. She followed the regiment that she had outlined and over the years, following the stroke, the pounds began to come off. Besides working out, Sharon danced at social settings at least twice a week. As she regained her figure she again became a magnet for both older and younger men and women. By the time she was 60, as the pounds dissipated, her figure took on a different dimension compared to what it had been in her youth. When she was fat, her buttocks grew to near enormous proportion. But as she lost the weight, her waist line shrunk and that left a curvature that accentuate her hips and butt. Men could not keep their eyes off of her behind. If she would have had breast she would she have been a Venus

One evening, while attending a steppers set, Sharon ran into Michael. Michael had to do a double take when he saw her. Sharon looked at Michel and recognized his confused gaze. They had met before when Sharon was fat and she knew that Michael was trying to process where he had seen her before. She helped him out "Hi, I'm Sharon. Don't you remember that we met at the venue on 22nd street a couple of years ago. "Oh yea "replied Michael. "I remember you. We danced a couple of times." What happened to you?   Dam! You sure got fine" He exclaimed. He couldn't help himself as he kept looking at Sharon with amazement. As they danced he stared at her and thought that she was so beautiful. He hardly could speak for looking at her. She helped him out by telling him that she had lost some weight and that this was her new look. Sharon asked Michael to keep dancing with her because she was trying to avoid a guy that she recently had a broken relationship with. She asked Michael to join her at her table so that the old boyfriend would see that she was occupied and thus would not bother her. Michael was elated to do so. Michael and Sharon danced all night and Michael proposed to take her to breakfast on the coming weekend.

To Michael surprise, Sharon began to have dates with him. He took her to dances, dinners and breakfasts and they spent time together at her house searching the Web. He could not believe that this fine woman was spending time with him. At the time that they met, (for the second time) Michael was 16 years older than Sharon. In his mid-seventies, he had relationships with women in his age bracket. There were plenty of woman in their sixties and seventies who wanted to be sexually active but they had no partners or their partners were not able to function sexually. Michael did not have that problem. He had relationships with from two to three women at any given time. The relationships were not romantic. They were sexual relationships. Michael made himself available upon being called by one of his older ladies when they wanted to make love.

Michael was dazzled by Sharon. He just wanted to be with her, look into her pretty, big black eyes, smell her aroma, watch her try on the dresses and cloths that he bought for her and to catch sight of her fabulous behind. He began to have a fixation on that body part. It was good that he was retired because his mind did not have room for many other thoughts except to think about Sharon. He thought about her all the time. He had not been much of a phone person, but he learned how to listen for the sound on his phone that alerted him to a text message from Sharon that would tell him that they could be together

Michael was financially secure for a man of his age. He had a life time of investments, savings, pension and social security. He was able and willing to help augment Sharon financially when she needed help. Sharon had prided herself at being financially independent but her fixed income became stressed when her expenses had an unexpected burden. Michael offered to help and Sharon accepted.   Michael felt good that he had come into Sharon's life when he could be of assistance to her. Finally, one day he made the assessment that - he was in love. How did this happen? Here he was in his seventies and he was in love. He searched his memory and could not remember that he had ever been in love before. He never had this feeling in the pit of his stomach that he would receive when the time came to see her. There had been plenty of woman in his life. There was a period when Michael had accepted a job in Atlanta, Georgia. He was in Atlanta for two years, in his mid-thirties, during the nineteen eighties. When in Atlanta, during that period, his was in the bars and taverns most ever night. When he left Atlanta, he could count nearly 50 woman he had been to bed with, but love had never entered his heart and now he was in love with and worshiping Sharon.   Notwithstanding, the fact that he was in love, Michael and Sharon had not been to bed until after they were 7 months into the relationship. Michael would request sex, but Sharon would not comply. Michael would have been gone if it had been any other woman. But his love for her kept him from pressuring her. He did not want to do anything to run her away. Sex took a back seat to love and besides he could get sex from his senior ladies when every he felt he had a need, which was now not often anymore. Having Sharon in his physical presence was all the climax that he needed.

Finally, after they had been companions for 8 months Sharon submitted to Michael advances. The sex was not that good. Michael felt that it was his fault. He was so mesmerized by laying naked with her that he felt that he was not as aggressive in bed with her as he usually was. The fact that Sharon made Michael use a condom did not help. He had never used a condo before and he could not feel his penis in her vagina because of the condom. But Michael did complete one fetish that he had developed since meeting Sharon. He got to kiss her behind.

About a week after their last sexual encounter (they only had two) Michael decided to go to a stepping affair (dance). Michael and Sharon had a set number of stepping affairs that they would go to together. This affair that Michael decided to go to was not one in which they would go together. Sharon had dances that she would also go to alone, as did Michael. Michael was sitting at a table between dances and as he looked toward the entrance door he saw Sharon come through the door and she was with a gentleman. They were arm and arm. Michael sat stunned as he looked at the couple take a seat at a table. He observed the couple in their seats displaying 'lovey - dovey' affection toward each other. Michael sat riveted in his chair. He couldn't believe his eyes. For a minute he believed his mind was playing tricks on him. "Was that really Sharon" he asked himself? He hadn't been staring but now he did. He took a hard, long look. Yes, that was Sharon.

Michael finally became unfrozen in his seat when a woman asked him to dance. As he danced with the woman he twirled her so that he could have a line of sight on Sharon and her man fiend. Michael never had a problem with sweating as he danced but he began to sweat profusely as he danced in this air-conditioned dance venue. As the dance with the woman ended, Michael again took his seat and he determined that he could use a cool drink. He rarely drank alcohol, but this was an occasion for a cool alcoholic drink. The blood that ran through his veins was pumping rapidly. It needed to be slowed down. He got up from his seat and walked to the bar and ordered a scotch and coke. He returned to his seat and swilled the refreshment quickly. He thought about getting another but decided he better not. He was not use to drinking and he recognized that he needed to keep his head together and besides that first drink had slowed his metabolism down. He sat at the table and kept his head down - staring at the blank wood on the table. In a low tone, under his breath he began talking to himself. "What did I do to her? Did I say something wrong? What did I do wrong? Why is she doing this to me?"

After a while, he decided to go and ask Sharon for a dance. He left his seat and proceeded to Sharon's location. He asked Sharon to dance with him. She indicated no by shaking her head and then looked away from Michael. She did not even speak to him. Michael turned and tucked his tail between his legs and left. He was hurt and embarrassed. We just fucked a week ago and now she won't even talk to me he thought to himself. "What did I do to deserve this he asked himself?" He felt that everyone in the joint was looking at him as he received the rejection from Sharon. As he walked back to his seat, the dejection that he had just experienced was mind boggling. He again set at his table trying to deal with his emotions, which were running wild. Finally, he could take it no more he got up and slithered out the door of the facility.

The hell in Michael's life began on that night. He was able to make it home. He sat on the side of his bed all night. He did not remove his cloths. Sleep would not visit him. He tried to ponder what had happened to him. He couldn't figure it out that night or any of the days and nights that followed. His normal method of communication with Sharon was through texting. He would text her. She would not respond. She must loath and despise me he thought. He went over in his mind what if anything he could have done to turn her against him. He could think of nothing He was bewildered and miserable He could not eat. He only ate when the state of his hunger was such that he was too weak to properly function. He would wolf something down and then continue with his misery. He longed to touch her. When he did get sleep it was for short periods. He would wake up and sit up in the middle of the bed and his heart would be beating fast upon waking. He had been dreaming about Sharon and the dream would not let him sleep.   He was in emotional pain. He wished for a good night's sleep, but it never came. He was at a point wherein he needed relief from this pain. He wanted to run away but he had no place to run to. He tried to belittle himself by telling himself that he was an old bastard that had no business being in love. After he was through belittling himself he would think of Sharon and was then back in his state of depression. He thought that maybe if this had not been the first time in his life that he was in love, this rejection would not have been so devastating, but it was

After a while, Sharon finally sent Michael a text. She indicated that she was dating and wanted to end their relationship. She listed all of the things that Michael had bought for her and the money he had given her. She thanked him and wished him luck. She had dropped him. He had wanted to hear from her, but that text blew his mind. He went into a deeper depression. He cut off all social interactions and either confined himself to his bed room or the couch in his living room to watch television.   He couldn't get Sharon out of his head.   He became fed up with himself. He thought that maybe if he could get Sharon to talk to him and tell him what he had done wrong, it would help.   He wasn't too proud to beg if that's what it took but he knew that begging her to talk would be stressful for her. Also, he had some pride left in him. So, he did not try to contact Sharon again. He had never been so lonesome. It was enough to make him lay down and die. He was mentally and emotionally exhausted. He was in a living nightmare because of his longing for Sharon. Oh! If he could only get some sleep - it would help. He Finally determined he wanted to end it all. He could not stand the thought that he would never get to hold Sharon again. He wished that he could go to sleep and never wake up. He didn't care about life anymore. He used to look down on people that committed suicide, but he was now ready to end his life so that the pain would end.

He had used prescription pills to get the little amount of sleep that he had received since he began this dilemma. He picked up the bottle on his nightstand and examined the contents. The bottle was three quarters full. He went to the refrigerator and got a bottle of cold water and returned to his bed. He took the pills from the bottle and began to swallow them - two at a time. When they began to take effect, he had swallowed 12 pills. He went to sleep, slumped across his bed.

In the morning, his wife attempted to rouse him, but no amount of shaking would awaken him. She looked at the bottle of pills that lay beside him and came to the conclusion that he had overdosed on what she knew were sleeping pills. She called 911. The ambulance came and based upon the information that the wife gave, the technicians put him in the ambulance and begin to prep him for the process of pumping his stomach when he got to the hospital. The ambulance alerted the hospital emergency room that a potential suicide victim was on the way and that the victim had ingested an overdose of sleeping pills. Upon arrival, between the emergency room and intensive care, the hospital did what was necessary to flush the overdosed medicine out of his system. He woke up in intensive care

When Michael work up it was like he was in a different world and he was a different man. He no longer had a feeling of anxiety. He had tubes sticking out of him that were providing life substances. He was calmer then he had ever been. He asked how he got where he was and was told by the hospital staff that they suspected that he had tried to commit suicide. The staff told him that he was near death when he came in, but he had been revived in the hospital. Slowly, it came back to him of the reason that he had tried to take his life. It was Sharon. But this time there was no sense of fretfulness when he raised her name. It was like Sharon had been ripped from his psyche. The hospital had pumped his stomach out and rid him of the drugs and Sharon had been pumped from him also. He was tranquil, peaceful and serene as he thought about her. He was good with the idea that he had experienced unrequited love. It's probably happened to millions of people, he thought but it was the first time that it happened to me and that's why he took it so hard. He rationalized that his whole experience was a human condition that many a man and a woman has suffered through. Some have reacted better than others. His ordeal was not the best way to handle being dumped. But he had no control over what had happened to his mentally. He hadn't violently confronted her. He alone had suffered the pain. Well at least he was alive and hopefully better for the experience. He was not going to give up on women. As soon as he was able, he was going to find himself a new beauty and romance but this time he would not fall in love. He felt fortunate that a man of his age had not given up on relations. As long as women would be attracted to him he would be attracted to women. He had a secret. He had an implant. He would be good until the day he died

Upon leaving the hospital, Michael thought two final things about Sharon. They both survived near death experiences and that <u>it was better to have loved her and lost than to never have loved at all.</u>

THE NEGLECTFUL NURSE

"Head Nurse for Three West. Head Nurse for Three West, report to your floor." The switch board operator repeated the message over the public-address system.

Lavern Carver had been in the cafeteria just long enough to have finished her sweet roll. She was about to relax with a cup of coffee when this intrusive notification blared out at her. The message that she heard had significance for her. She was being summoned back to her floor. Lavern was the head nurse on Three West at Washington Community Hospital located on the west side of Chicago.

She cursed under her breath and capped her coffee and pushed away from the cafeteria table.

"You're not losing another one?" asked Rene Lumpkin, a pharmacist who was taking her break at the next table. She was referring to the fact that two patients had died on Three West last week.

"No nothing like that," replied Nurse Carver. "I've got a couple of rookies on duty. They're just out of nursing school. We've got a patient returning from surgery. I told them to page me when they brought him back to the floor. I want to make sure that those neophytes don't stick the I.V. in his behind instead of his arm."

Rene laughed and said. "yeah, I know what you mean. Last week a graduate nurse on Two South mixed up a pharmaceutical order for estrogen supplement. She had it ordered for a male patient. I make sure that I double check the orders from the floor that I know rookies have been hired on."

"Keep doing that," Nurse Carver instructed as she moved away from the table. "It will help keep the malpractice suits away and it might save someone's life. See you later."

She gestured her hand in a waving goodbye motion to Lumpkin and moved through the cafeteria doors. Her hands smoothed out the wrinkles in her immaculate white nurse's uniform as she walked to the elevator. At 5 feet 6 inches tall, she was a stately looking nurse with an athletic build. A peek at her watch indicated that it was just ten o'clock. She thought to herself that the anesthesiologist must have cut the juice (anesthetic) this morning. She did not expect Mr. Boyles back from post op until 10:30. It would have been nice to have been able to finish her coffee. She promised herself that she would make up for the missed break by leaving a little early today. I will not be working ten hours today like I've been doing all week, she gleeful thought.

"Nina my daughter and grand babies will be here tonight" she said with gusto, out loud.

It was loud enough to be heard by people who were exiting the elevator, as the door flew open – at the tail end of her statement. The people leaving the elevator, looked at Nurse Carver as if she was a little crazy for talking to herself. Lavern felt a bit self-conscious for having got caught chattering with herself. What the Hell! She was feeling good. She hadn't seen her babies in a long time.

The elevator doors closed, and she was alone ascending to the third floor. She had a moment to reflect on what she would do for the rest of the day. She was short staffed on the day shift. She had only the two new registered nurses, two LPNs (Licensed Practical Nurses), three aids and a ward clerk to work the twenty-bed unit. She would probably have to do a lot of hands on nursing – no time to work the reports that were near due. She recalled that she was supposed to attend an infection control committee meeting that afternoon. She would call the Director of Nursing and leave word for the committee not to expect her attendance. She had nine patients on her medical surgical unit who had had surgery within the last two days. They were doing fine but the new nurses were a little skittish of them. She would work closely with her new staff until they got their confidence. The nurses had only been out of orientation a couple of weeks. They needed a little more time before they were capable of handling the rigors of nursing without a mother hen watching closely over them.

Lavern stepped off the elevator half expecting chaos on her floor. Everything appeared to be running smoothly. There was a beehive of activity occurring. An x-ray technologist was wheeling a patient to the radiology department. He had stopped at the nursing station to flirt with the ward clerk. Upon seeing Nurse Carver, he pretended to be getting some information on his patient - he moved on. It was time for the vampires (Lab technicians). They were making their rounds to draw their daily supply of blood from the patients. The physical therapy department had a couple of representatives on the floor. They were there to collect Mrs. Reed from room 304. She had a spinal injury received in a car accident. They would take her to their labyrinth located in the corner of the basement. There she would resume the work started toward restoring her body to a level of functioning that would allow her to lead a somewhat less than normal life.

"Hi, how are you doing today?" asked Nurse Carver of Gladys Reed as they wheeled her past the head nurse.

"Just fine but I could sleep in today. These guys are so persistent about me doing my work," answered Mrs. Reed.

"You got to get strong so that you can go home," said Nurse Carver.

"I don't' know if it's worth all of the work. I don't seem to be getting any better," replied the patient.

"I'll stop by and chat with you later this afternoon," Nurse Carver said with a worried expression on her face. Carver thought Gladys Reed seemed to be getting depressed. She was not making the kind of progress that was hoped for. Laverne Carver resolved to talk to Mrs. Reed's doctor when he visited today. She wondered had he observed the signs of depression that she saw.

Out of the corner of her eye, The Head Nurse observed every action on her floor as she proceeded down the corridor toward the patient's room who had returned from the OR. One of the LPN's was on her cell phone in a patient room. Cell phone usage was not allowed by staff while on duty. Nurse Carver would deal with her after she checked on Mr. Boyles.

"I'm going home today boss lady," announced an aggressive robust young man standing in the doorway of his room, as he saw the head nurse approaching.

Johnnie Wilson had come into the hospital through the emergency room. He had been operated on for gunshot wounds in the abdomen. Gunshot wounds were routine at Washington Community hospital. The hospital surgeons had a lot of practice mending the shooting victims on the west side of Chicago where the Hospital was located. Despite the fact that the doctors repaired his stomach, Johnnie almost died. He developed pneumonia. He had to have his lungs pumped to save his life. He was ok now, and he was rearing to get out and go back to the streets.

"We'll see what your doctor has to say," replied the Head Nurse as she walked past his room.

She hoped that he would be able to go home today. It always made her nervous to have gang members on her ward. Those macho young men and their visitors were capable of doing anything. She didn't take any stuff from them nor would she allow her staff to take their crap. When they came on her ward she would lay down the law. Her bluff had most often worked. She rarely had to call security for the gangs. She most often had to call security for domestic altercations. Like when a wife caught her husband's girlfriend visiting him. But Lavern Carver was afraid of the gangs. Being a southern girl, she just was not use to young boys being so grown up and unmanageable. She never got over the time when a fifteen-year-old gang banger who was visiting his friend told her "Momma you sure look good to me. I'd like to swap your spit."

She reached Mr. Broyles' room. Both new nurses were settling the patient in. He had undergone surgery for a hernia. The doctors could not perform the new noninvasive laparoscopic procedure to repair the tear. The had to cut him to mend the rupture in the wall of his intestinal cavity. He came out of the influence of anesthesia in recovery, but the nurses were now seeing to it that he was comfortable after he was received back in his room. He was starting to experience some pain. Carver entered just as one of the nurses was about to administer medication in his IV to relieve the discomfort. The nurse saw Carver and stopped.

"Go on," ordered the Head Nurse. "He's been back to the floor long enough to give him that medication".

"We were trying to wait for you," replied the other rookie nurse.

"Do what your training taught you," she instructed, as The Head Nurse inspected the surgeon's work. "Mr. Boyles, how do you feel?" asked Nurse Carver.

He answered weakly, "it's beginning to hurt."

"You'll be alright in a minute. We're giving you some Demerol for the pain," said Nurse Carver. "Did you take his vital signs?" the Head Nurse asked.

"Yes," was the response that she received.

"Good! You can go on and attend to your other assigned patients. I'll make Mr. Boyles comfortable."

As the nurses were leaving, Carver was telling the patient that he was catheterized and what that meant. It was explained to him that he would remain so for a day or two depending on how he progressed. She also explained to him that he was being fed intravenously and enlightened him on the particulars of his condition. She stayed with the patient until the pain subsided, and he was about to fall asleep.

When she left Mr. Broyles' room, she looked for and found the LPN that was on her cell phone in the patient room. She would not accept any excuse given by her employee to be on that phone. She warned her that a suspension would be given if another infraction occurred.

The rest of nurse Carver's day was spent at a steady pace – taking care of patient business. There was a lot of business to take care of. Admitting patients to her floor, conferring with doctors, directing staff and answering question for patients and their families engaged her through the day. She also managed to do some paper work.

You couldn't be a head nurse at Washington Community Hospital and be one that gets flustered. If something could go wrong - it would go wrong on the wards of that institution. The facility was old, therefore there always was something going wrong with the heating, plumbing or the electrical system. The breakdown of one of those system effected either the care or the comfort of her patients. Lavern Carver was committed to quality care. She was adept at dealing with other department heads to solve the problems on her ward. She was the kind of head nurse that made others involved in the delivery of patient care more efficient either because they were glad to contribute or because they feared her wrath.

The Hospital had been striving to improve its reputation for care. The perception of the hospital being a place to receive good care in the community had suffered since the hospital's clients became mostly Black. That happened when the community changed from White to Black in the sixties. Until recently, the hospital could only attract public aide patients who had no choice. Ten years ago, the hospital made a conscious effort to improve its reputation. A Director of Nursing that was known for delivering quality care was hired. She in turn hired head nurses like Lavern Carver who had been a head nurse at prestigious Chicago hospitals. Slowly but surely, the community was gaining confidence in the facility. New physicians were being attracted to the staff and private insurance patients were being admitted. The present Director of Nursing was about to retire, and everyone knew that Nurse Carver was the 'Heir apparent'. Lavern Carver at 51, was looking forward to the challenge. She wanted to make an overall contribution to nursing care in the Black community.

At about 2:00 PM, she received a telephone call at the nursing station. Her daughter, Nina, was on the other end of the line.

"Hi Mom. We just got in. I've got your grand babies at the airport."

"Hi Baby! Did you have a good trip? How did the babies like the airplane?"

"Fine mom. They slept most of the time. They made out better than me. You know that I don't like to fly."

"Is your father there yet?"

"Yes, he's here. I just wanted to call you when we got in. I know that you were worried about your grandbabies."

"I was worried about you too baby. Tell your father to bring you home. I'll be there shortly after you get there."

"OK Mom. See you later."

Lavern Carver hung up the phone and light-heartedly finished her shift. She figured that her husband would have the girls (daughter and granddaughters) home in about an hour. She would be home within a half hour after they arrived. As she gave report to the nurses that were relieving her, they could see that she was excited about her children's visit. Lavern had no idea of the twist of fate that would come about as a result of her daughters visit.

Eighteen Months Later

Lavern Carver was sitting in the outer office of the administrator of Jackson Memorial Hospital in Atlanta Georgia. She was now living in Atlanta and was employed at this hospital. She had been summoned to a meeting. Her Head Nurse, the Director of Nursing, The Personnel Director and the Hospital Attorney were also waiting to be called into the office for the meeting. Lavern Carver looked haggard and drawn. Her uniform which was not fresh, ill fitted her and her nurse's white shoes could have used some polish. She had let her hair turn partially grey and it hadn't been done in - who knows when. It was just combed straight back. As she sat and waited, she held her head cradled in one hand, turning it from one side to the other. She was being watched by the others in the office. There was pity in their look. She did not look at them. Her eyes were closed most of the time that she waited. The door to the Administrators office opened. He invited everybody in. Once they were seated, he started the meeting.

The Administrator informed Ms. Carver that an investigation had been going on for some time. Nurse Carver was the focus of the investigation. She had been suspected of stealing patient narcotic medication. The medicine cabinet came up short when she was in charge and patients who were in her care complained about pain in too quick intervals after receiving their pain killing shots. This was an indication that their recommended medication strength could have been cut. The Hospital indicated that it had determined that Lavern Carver was in a position to commit those infractions. Nurse Carver was asked to voluntarily take a drug test. She refused. Her Head Nurse then stated a litany of evidence that had been compiled against her. Lavern Carver was asked to defend herself against the charges that were being made. She weakly denied the charges but did not vigorously defend herself. She gave every appearance of wanting the session to be over with. The personnel Director then indicated that she was being suspended pending further investigation. The Hospital Attorney told her that if the Hospital found the charges to be true, they would turn over the evidence to the State Department of Registration in order that they revoke her nursing license. The Director of Nursing counseled her to seek professional help if she had a drug problem. She was notified that the investigation would be over within two days and she would be notified of the results.

Lavern Carver gathered her belongings and left the hospital and headed for a bar that she began to frequent since coming to Atlanta. She had a couple of drinks – was about to buy another when she thought better of it. She has almost had a car accident in the past when she did her drinking on the street.

She bought a fifth to take home and left. Once home, she sat at her kitchen table and began to drink and cry. The crying was not about the hospital meeting that had happened that afternoon. She was really glad that they found out about what she had been doing. She was hooked on drugs. She knew that, and she also knew that she wasn't a good nurse anymore. She could have been the cause of someone's death if she continued. Now she would not have to leave the apartment except to buy liquor and some food.

All of a sudden, the thought hit her that since she would no longer be at the hospital she no longer could keep herself supplied with drugs. She needed the drugs. They made her sleep. She needed to sleep. When she slept the pain would go away. The pain was what she was crying about. When she slept the pain would go away. Lavern had a whole lot of pain. The pain was mental agony and anguish. The drugs made her pain bearable. Liquor only made her drunk and sick. She would have to find another source for her drugs. She had before been approached in the bar to buy drugs. She would attempt to establish a contact tomorrow.

She got up from the kitchen table and fumbled into the living room. The television had been turned on when she came into the apartment. Her living quarters consisted of a kitchen, living room, a bath and her bedroom. It was small. It looked smaller then it was because Lavern did not pick up after herself. She had lost the fastidious quality that she had had all of her life. Her place looked like a pigsty. Lavern was oblivious to it. She pushed aside some food containers from a past fast food meal and sat on the couch. Her uniform had been pulled down around her waist exposing her bra. She was drinking straight from the bottle. Sleep wouldn't come to her. if she had her drugs, she would have been unconscious by now. She wanted to pass out. She drank more but it couldn't render her insensible. The painful thoughts that she was trying to black out were creeping back into her brain. She couldn't keep them away. They had to be dealt with tonight. Her hands pressed tightly against her head as if to give one last ditch effort to suppress those thoughts. It didn't work. The events of the last eighteen months danced before her.

Flashback

She remembered how elated she was when she saw her daughter and grand babies as they visited her. They stayed with her for a week.

What a good time they had. She hugged and kissed those babies to death. She managed to take off from work two days and they went to the zoo and to a children's museum. She lavished all of her affection on her grandchildren. She didn't pay enough attention on her daughter. I don't think that I kissed her once she thought, except when she first greeted her at the house. I should have been more observant of her. "Oh god. Why wasn't I," she asked talking to herself. Lavern hated it when the visit was over. It meant the she had to again part with her favorites. She put them on the plane and promised to come visit them in their home in Philadelphia that summer. Her daughter was not feeling well when the plane took off.

The next day while at work, Lavern received a call from her husband, Ray. He told her that Nina's husband had called and informed him that Nina had taken sick on the plane. She was taken by ambulance to the hospital after the plane landed.

"What's wrong with her?" Lavern asked.

"They don't know. Bill, Nina's husband, said that they were running tests. He's at the hospital in her room waiting for the results," was the answer given by Lavern's husband.

Lavern called the hospital in Philadelphia and was connected to her daughter's room. Nina's husband answered the phone. He told her that Nina had been unconscious since she arrived at the hospital. She was having a hard time breathing. He said that he had wanted to call last night but he had to make arrangements for someone to take care of the girls.

"She wasn't feeling well when she left but I had no indications that she was that sick" Lavern told her son-in-law. "Do you think that I should come?" she asked.

"The girls are with my sister. I don't know if you should make the trip" he responded. "I think that we ought to wait a little while before we do anything. She probably will come around. The test results will be back soon. I'm waiting to talk to the doctor. I'll call you as soon as

I get some information," he indicated.

"All right," answered Lavern. "But call me as soon as you know something." Lavern gave him the number.

She tried to continue to perform her duties, but her mind was with her sick daughter. About an hour after she got off of the phone with her son-in-law, he called again.

"Hi Mom, Nina has gotten worst. They are going to put her on a respirator. The doctor thinks that she has some kind of influenza that combined with pneumonia. Maybe you better come."

Terror shot through Lavern. "I'll catch the first plane available; I hope I can get there tonight if I can catch a flight."

Lavern called and was able to reserve an evening flight to Philadelphia. She made arrangement to be away from work for an indefinite period. She called her other daughter who lived in St Louis and told her of her sister's condition. She threw some essentials into an overnight bag and left the house. Lavern's husband could not accompany her to Philadelphia, but he took her to the airport and comforted her while she waited for the plane. He would come if Nina's condition did not improve.

The flight to Philadelphia was not fast enough for Lavern. When she arrived, she got a cab and went straight to the hospital. Upon arrival, she joined her son-in-law in what amounted to a death watch of her daughter. Nina passed away that night.

It happened so fast that it numbed Lavern's senses, but her nursing experience automatically surged into play. Her son-in-law cried like a baby. Lavern consoled him that night at the hospital. She had experienced the death of her parents and had helped her family cope with that calamity. Even though it was her daughter, she knew that she had to be strong for the whole family. The next day she broke the word to her grandchildren. Telling them that their mother was with God. How do you explain to children that their healthy twenty-five-year-old mother who was loving them days ago is now gone?

Lavern nurtured her grandchildren and the whole family, on both sides during that time. She and her other daughter, Theresa, joined her in assisting the son-in-law make the arrangements and taking care of family member that came for the funeral. Nina's husband was not able to perform that function. He was grief stricken. Lavern only broke down and cried when they placed the body of her daughter in the ground at the cemetery.

Lavern stayed in Philadelphia for two weeks after the funeral. She helped her son-in-law to establish a routine for her grandchildren. His family was from Philadelphia. He and her daughter had met while they attended college in the south. They married and settled in his home town. They were both teachers in the Philadelphia school system. Lavern told her son-in-law that she wanted to keep the grandchildren for a short time. She had to go back to work but after a few weeks she intended to take a couple of weeks off. That time was going to be set aside for those little ones.

"I'll call you when I get back home, and we can be more definite about the time frame," she told him.

"Ok, Mom. We'll talk about it," he said. He and his daughters kissed her as they put her on the plane for Chicago.

Lavern resumed her work upon returning home. She now also had time to grieve her daughter. She grieved her in a quite dignified way. She cried for her when she was alone. Her heart longed for her when she came across an item that she associated with Nina. She could be in the middle of something – anything– and her thoughts would focus on her daughter. It took all of her strong will and strength to continue doing what she was doing. It had been hard enough that both of her daughters had chosen to marry and move out of the city but, at least she was able to see them on occasions. It was difficult to accept the fact that she would never see Nina again. Her husband consoled and helped her during this time of grief. Ray Carver was not the father of the two girls. Lavern had a previous marriage. The girls were the product of that first marriage. The marriage did not last long. She divorced and met Ray when the girls were six and seven years old. The girls' father was never a part of their life. Nina was the oldest. She and Ray had raised two fine girls who both graduated from college and were embarked with careers and with families. Theresa, her youngest daughter, also had a child.

Lavern kept in constant contact with her son-in-law over the next three weeks. She wanted to make sure he and the girls were well as they could be under the circumstances. Her desire to keep the kids for a while grew stronger and she began to press for a date from Bill in order that she could make arrangements to take a vacation. Bill seemed hesitant to agree to a date or even to the arrangement. He kept putting her off from one week to the next. He would make an excuse not to accommodate her. She called him three times during one week, trying to get him to commit. At first, she excused his inability to commit as a result of his trying to bring some normalcy to his life but then wonder entered her mind. Was there some reason that her son-in law did not want her to keep the kids for a while? She confronted him with that question the next time that she called him.

"Bill, I sense that you do not want me to keep the kids. You know that I will take good care of them."

"No Mom, it's not that. I have every confidence in your ability to care for them. It's just that the kids and I are trying to adjust. It might be too soon to put them in another environment." he stated.

Lavern was hurt by that "another environment" comment but she didn't harp on it. In the ensuing weeks she was still persistent about having the kids. Every week she was on the phone with Bill. Finally, she could take it no more.

She asked Bill, "Do you have a problem with me? I always thought that we got along well. I never interfered with your and Nina's lives…"

Bill cut her off, "Mom It's nothing like that. I have the highest regard and respect for you. It's not that."

"Well what is it?"

"Well, it's nothing to do with you."

"Well, what's it to do with then?"

"Mom I really hoped to avoid this...but I see I can't...Maybe it's best that I tell you because I really think that you need to know. It's about Ray."

"Ray! What's Ray got to do with this?"

"Mom, I have to tell you this because you have to believe that I trust you and that I want the kids to cherish and love you. Nina told me that...that she had been sexually abused by Ray when she was young ...both she and Theresa."

"What! What are you saying Bill?"

"Mom, that's what Nina said. We never told you, but Nina had to have therapy because of it. She would have never told you, but this came up because of the kids...and now.... well I got to tell you why I don't want the girls to come. I know you couldn't be around them and protect them all of the time when they come to visit."

Lavern's heart felt like it was taking a ride down on a fast-moving elevator. It landed with a thud on the lowest floor. Her blood rushed to her head at the same time. She could not believe this incredulous, vicious statement from Bill. She thought, why would he tell this perverse lie to keep the babies from me? Bill continued to tell Lavern all that Nina had related to him about the abuse. He told her that the girls were abused at night when Lavern was working the night shifts. Ray would get them out of bed and engage them in sexual play of all kinds. As young girls, Nina and Theresa thought it was fun. Ray made them believe that it was their secret. The games stopped when the girls were about 12 and 13 years old. Nina told Bill that it began to bother

her when she got about 15 years old. She then knew that it had been wrong, but she couldn't tell you because she thought that it was her fault too. Theresa had confirmed Nina's story when she came to visit.

"Nina felt guilty. She would never have told you. She made me promise to never tell you…But things are different now and I had to tell you," said Bill.

After getting off the phone with Bill, Lavern had a sense of panic. She was known to be one cool cookie, but coolness was not with her now. Her memory failed her as she tried to dial her daughter's number in St Louis. She had to look the number up in her telephone book. She dialed it.

"Theresa!"

"Hi Mon! How you doing?"

"I just got through talking to Bill. He said something to me that was very disturbing."

"Yeah. What Mom?"

"He said that Ray had sexually abused you and Nina when you were young, and he said that you told him that it was true. You didn't tell him that. Did you"?

"Oh boy! Mom…Jesus...Dam…I wish he hadn't said anything to you about that."

"What do you mean, you wish he…Is it true or not…Did you or not tell him that your father molested you?"

"Well …yeah Mom it's true. Dad did…bother us when we were young."

"Girl, what are you saying? You never said anything to me about this."

"Yeah Mom. I know I didn't. I couldn't. I don't believe Bill would do this. He promised he wouldn't."

"What do you mean he shouldn't have told me. Somebody better tell me something. I'm beginning to feel like a fool. You better talk to me Theresa!"

Theresa began to talk. The conversation went on and on. The mother and daughter finally, painfully exploring a part of their life that had not been shared before. It was the most important and stressful conversation that Lavern had ever had with her daughter. Initially, Lavern blamed her daughter for not telling her. The daughter successfully explained that she and her sister were too young. They were confused. When they were old enough to know what happened to them was wrong, they felt guilty about it. The guilt followed them into adulthood. Theresa told her mother that she also had to have therapy.

Lavern pressed Theresa for all the details of the abuse. Theresa did not want to give them up, but she could not withstand the pressure that was being applied by her mother. After giving some details, Theresa begin crying and requested that her mother discontinue the probing conversation. Theresa explained that she had been through her period of fault and shame. She was past her crisis and had moved on with her life. Lavern persisted in her inquiry. Theresa became angry with her mother.

The daughter then firmly told her mother, "Mom, I wish that you had never found out but now that you know, you will have to deal with that knowledge like Nina and I had to deal with the aftermath of the abuse. But don't blame Nina and I for what happened. You were our mother and you did not protect us. I can't and will not talk about it anymore. You are bringing back a painful part that I do not want to deal with again. I put my demons to rest. You are going to have to deal with yours. I am going to say goodbye for now. We will talk again some other time. Goodbye Mom. I'll call you next week, but I cannot, at this time deal with this." With that she hung up.

Lavern sat with the phone in her hand for a long time, just staring ahead. At that point she knew that her life would never be the same.

She felt empty, worthless, crushed. Lavern Carver big shot Head Nurse, who had all the answers for everybody else, didn't even know what happened under her own roof. Her daughter's words kept ringing over and over 'you were our mother and you did not protect us' She wanted to scream, run, do something, anything. This was a bad dream. No, it wasn't. I couldn't wake up and it would be over, she thought. She was already awake. She fought with her emotions until her husband came home from work. Theirs had been a good relationship for twenty plus years.

"You Black bastard," she greeted him as he came through the door.

You can imagine that Ray was taken off guard by that greeting. They never had harsh words. They were a middle age couple that had an ideal relationship. For an instant, Ray thought that Lavern was playing with him. She then called him an incestuous, pedophilic Black bastard. The meaning of the words did not connect. He wasn't intellectual. Ray was a foreman on an assembly line at an automobile plant. Though the meaning of the words did not mesh, how she said them conveyed the message that she was not being playful with him. She pressed forward with the attack.

"You took advantage of my daughters. How could you...sexually...molest my babies?" she asked with revulsion in her voice.

Her hands were now on her hips and her head was bobbing to the rhythm of her speech. It had happened so long ago that Ray had put it out of mind. He had forgotten about the past secret transgression against Lavern's daughters. Lavern jogged his memory with the details that had been given to her that afternoon by Bill and Theresa. She was livid with rage as she pounded away at this person that had shared her house and her bed for much of her life. Ray denied that he had committed the acts that he was being accused of. He only admitted that the girls would often come into the bedroom and sit on his lap.

"They was fast little girls then. They use to wiggle around on my lap when they did that," he said.

29

"And you, you, you sick bastard felt obliged to run your hand under their nighties. You blamed little babies for your weirdo sexual pervasion for little children," was the retort that Lavern gave.

Lavern continued to accuse, confront and verbally assault Ray about his molestation. Ray's best defense of himself was to hunch his shoulders, stick his hands out, palms upward and say, "baby whatever the girls thought happened and I ain't saying that anything happened…well it was years ago Why you want to bring up that shit now?"

Lavern responded by telling him that "I should call the god damn police and have your ass locked up but my behind should also go…for being so dumb as to allow it to happen."

She raged on with him until she was too physically and emotionally exhausted to persist any further. She walked away from the confrontation and went to a room in the house that she used for sewing and reading. Her mind was still in a frenzy. She just sat and stared at the wall trying to focus on what to do After about an hour had passed, Ray knocked on the door.

"Lavern Baby, did you cook anything to eat?" he asked softly.

After a pause, Lavern's answer came back. "Nigger you don't ever in life want to eat anything that I cook because it will be your last meal."

Thereafter, Lavern and Ray only communicated when they had to take care of business matters of the household. She moved out of the bedroom into her sewing room. Lavern tried to adjust her life so that she would only be home when it was time to go to bed. She stayed at work for long hours. Although Lavern stayed at work for long hours, she was really working less at working and directing the activities of her staff then she had previously been. She stayed in her office most of the time. She only left the office when it was absolutely necessary to do so. Her nurses were left more and more to use their own judgment to solve problems on her floor They became apprehensive about disturbing her office sanctuary. She was visibly agitated when she had to leave that refuge and she appeared to be becoming detached from people and nursing issues. She was being consumed with guilt and a loss of self-worth. She was also losing the emotion and attention to detail that she always had for her profession. Her nurses and the Director of Nursing Administration attributed her behavior to the post-traumatic stress of losing her daughter. They would give her time to overcome her loss. The nurses took up the slack. It was at this time that Lavern began to steal and use valium from the medicine cabinet. She needed it to make her sleep. Every waking minute was torture. Sleep sought relief.

Lavern went from loving Ray to loathing him. She seriously thought about killing him to revenge the perversion that he had visited upon her daughters. She could not bring herself to take his life. The decision made her feel like a coward and further depressed her. She did decide that she no longer could live under the same roof with the man who had debased her children. She would leave him.

Lavern was basely an inhibited woman, conservative and restrained. Therefore, she had few friends and there were only two or three people who she felt close with. Her daughters, especially Nina, had been her best friends. Now, she couldn't bring herself to talk to Theresa. They had not talked since that fateful phone conversation. She would be embarrassed to share this secret with anyone. But Lavern became paranoid in that she began to suspect that people knew that she had been a neglectful mother and had let something terrible happen to her children. As her paranoia and hate for Ray increased, she began to use more drugs obtained illegally from the hospital to calm herself and to make her sleep.

A plan began to develop to relieve her misery. First, she needed to get away from Ray. Get him out of her life – quick. There were days at home when she did not see him, but she could hear him and that made her skin creep. She didn't want to go through any long drawn out divorce proceedings that might bring to light the cause of their break up. No negotiations about things and money. She just wanted to drop out of his life, like she had never been a part of it. There would be no fight about the house and whatever material things they had accumulated. He could have it all. She did not want anything that would remind her of him. She did not intend to negotiate about money nor did she intend for him to have the money that they had accumulated. There was a considerable amount of that. Fortunately, Lavern had set up and controlled the family finances. She paid the bills and her signature was on the bank accounts. There was cash in the bank and they also had certificates of deposit (CD). Counting the CDs, there was over one hundred thousand dollars that was available. Lavern also had an annuity and a 401k pension plan at work which she intended to cash in. She developed plans to leave Chicago. She wanted a complete break with their past. She knew that a nurse could get a job anywhere in the country.

After thinking about a city to settle in, Lavern decided on Atlanta, Georgia. That city was chosen because Lavern was originally from a small town in Georgia. As a small girl her parents had taken her to Atlanta for visits and she had dreamed of living in Atlanta one day. The family moved to Chicago when she was fourteen and she had never been back to Georgia since she was a youngster. Yes, Atlanta was big enough to get lost in and she could still earn a living.

Lavern laid definite plans for her getaway. She tendered her resignation at the hospital and gave a thirty-day notice. The hospital administrator expressed sadness upon receiving the letter of resignation. Lavern Carver was to be the next director of nursing. Although sadness was expressed, the administrator felt relieved. Nurse Carver was not the same efficient Head Nurse that she had been just a few months prior. If he had to make the decision to appoint her today, he probably would have chosen someone else. He wasn't even aware nor in any way suspected that Nurse Carver had developed a drug habit as a result of stealing narcotics from the patient medication.

Lavern applied for her pension and annuity money at work. The paper work would take some time to process and Lavern indicated to the Plan Administrator that she would contact them in order that the checks could be sent to a post office box in Atlanta which she would establish when she got to that city. On the morning after her resignation from the hospital, she intended to leave town with just her cloths, some personal effects, her car and her money.

While Ray was at work, she packed what she was going to take in her car and left. The day before she had gone to the bank and got a cashier check for over one hundred thousand dollars. She left ten thousand dollars in the account. Ray was also left a letter telling him of the deepness of her alienation toward him and that it was best she left before she took either his or her life. She told him that she had taken the money but that he had the house, the furniture and everything else, a fair exchange. She did not notify any other person or member of her family that she was leaving.

Two days later Lavern arrived in Atlanta. She checked into a hotel and stayed until she located an apartment. She could readily see, from going on line at the library and looking at health care sites, that finding a job was not going to be a problem. Nurses were in demand in Atlanta as they were across the nation. A nursing licensee in Illinois is changeable for a licensee in Georgia. After Lavern got her apartment, she applied for the transfer of her licensee and when that was accomplished she then began interviewing for nursing jobs. She was in no hurry to find work because not working allowed her to escape into her world of drug induced sleep and she had money. She bought a good supply of narcotics from Chicago with her that she had acquired from her hospital in Chicago and it was only after her supply became low that she accepted one of the many offers that she had. Her initial nursing position was not at Jackson Memorial Hospital. She had worked six months at another hospital. Nurse Carver left that hospital when she found out that her unit was being investigated because there was a shortage of narcotics medication that could not be accounted for. Lavern thus applied for and was hired at Jackson Memorial Hospital. While at Jackson Memorial Hospital, her narcotics habit developed to the extent that she lost her ability to be cautious and to hide her theft. Thus, the hospital developed a prima facie case against her and had conducted the meeting that afternoon.

———

Lavern's recall of the events that occurred since the death of her daughter ended with her passing out from the effects of the alcohol that she consumed. She slept a good length of time but woke feeling sick as a dog. She was hung over and craved for the narcotics that she was accustomed to having. Lavern searched the apartment to try and find remnants of drugs that she had ingested. Only a few valium tablets were found. She was never able to have a large reserve supply at home because only small amounts at a time could be appropriated from patient supplies. Lavern was used to having access to the drugs Morphine, Demerol and Valium. Those drugs were used in hospitals to thwart patient pain and to relieve stress. Morphine and Demerol all were injectable drugs. Valium is taken by mouth. Because she had access to those powerful addictive drugs, through her job, she never had to go out looking to procure narcotics. Now, that she would not be working, she had to find another source. She knew that she would probably not be able to purchase morphine or Demerol on the street. She hoped to be able to buy heroin, which was close to the drug that she had become accustomed to. It took all of her strength to get dressed and make herself presentable so that she could venture out to look for a drug buy.

It was early afternoon when Lavern arrived at the bar that she had been stopping at after work. She was surprised to find that it was half full during that time of day. She bought a drink and began gazing around looking for a young man who had once approached her in an effort to sell her drugs. He had been in the bar often when she stopped in to have a drink. She did not see him. He had not told her his name, so she couldn't ask for him unless she asked for the guy that sold drugs. She had better sense than to do that even though she was getting desperate. After a while, he did come in. He was not a menacing looking young man. He didn't even look like the typical young Black man of his day. His head was not clean shaven. He had a full head of hair. He wore blue jeans that were creased and pressed and instead of a t-shirt with some sports logo on it, he wore a short sleeve sport shirt that looked freshly laundered. The trade mark gym shoes of the young did not adorn the feet of this youngster. Skinny at 5 feet 10 inches, he didn't look old enough to be in a bar. Lavern was hesitant about going up to him. She pretended to be going to the wash room and as she passed him she asked would he join her when she returned from the ladies room. He did as requested when she returned.

As he slid next to her he asked, "what's up lady?"

In a professional like manner – with lowered voice – Lavern stated, "some time ago you asked me did I want to buy something that you had to sell. I didn't, at the time. I do now."

"Yeah baby and what would that be?" the young man asked in a wary manner.

Lavern whispered, "I want to buy some drugs."

He leaned back on the bar stool and gave a long hard look. His gaze made her uncomfortable. She was already on pins and needles. – her habit had come down on her. If she wouldn't have been in such bad shape, she would never imagine having a conversation with this young man from this street. After what appeared to be an eternity, the young man's apprehension seemed to disappear. He told her he had seen her come into the bar a number of times but he thought that she was a lush head – only. He didn't know that she was into crack. Lavern knew what crack was. She hadn't seen it but like most every other American had heard about it.

"No, I'm looking for some heroin," she told him.

He leaned over to her and said in a hushed voice, "Whoa baby. I ain't got no heroin. I only deal cocaine and weed. So you use heroin?" he asked.

"No, I never used it," answered Lavern.

"Mama you want to start using some powerful shit," the young man told her with a puzzled look on his face.

To this point neither had introduced themselves. She asked his name. He told her to call him Tommie.

"I'm Miss Carver." She gave him her real name.

Lavern asked if he knew anyone who could sell her the heroin. Tommie told her that he knew a dude that sold the stuff, but it might take a couple of days to get in touch with him.

Tommie asked, "You ain't never had no cocaine?"

"No," replied Lavern.

The young man began to sense that Lavern needed something bad. He had an experienced eye for a hype. He began to push the exalted effects of cocaine on her. Tommie told her that he had crack and the powdered cocaine. He didn't have to push real hard.

"What does it look like?" asked Lavern

Tommie said, "Shit baby. I don't carry the stuff on me. It's in my stash."

He was right. she did need something – bad. He could make a sale. If it was safe.

"I've never used that. Do you think that it will do for me what I need done?" asked Lavern.

"Yeah Baby. It will make you feel smoother then a baby's butt," replied Tommie.

There was only one problem Lavern didn't know how to use it. Lavern cast her eyes upward from her hands that she had been wringing and said, "I don't know how to use it. Will you show me?"

Tommie looked at her with a puzzled expression on his face. He had never had a customer ask him to instruct them in the use of the substance that he sold.

"Well Mama all you got to do is cook it and snort it or inject it," he told her with impatience creeping into his voice.

Again, Lavern asked, "will you show me how to use it?"

"Damn Baby! Where I'm gonna show you? Here in the street? You gotta be out of your mind!"

"No, you can show me at my place I'll pay you."

Tommie became apprehensive at this point. He began to wonder whether this broad was a plant. He recalled that he had seen her come into the joint many times before in the recent past. She would get near drunk and then leave. He couldn't ever remember seeing her talking with anybody. No one really knew nothing about this old lady. He thought that she was a maid or cook because he always saw her with a white uniform under her coat. Could she be some kind of cop set up? No one had ever offered to pay to show them how to do the do. Some broads tried to trade sex for drugs, but they were young hypes. This old lady didn't look like…well he didn't know what she did or didn't look like. She just wasn't the run of the mill type that he sold drugs to. She kind of looked like his mother.

Tommie was a relatively successful street level pusher. At 21 years old, he cleared 8 to 9 hundred dollars per week in drug sales. That amounted to 50,000 per year – tax free. He had been selling dope since he was seventeen. He attributed his success to the fact that he worked hard to develop his customer base. He was a loner, cautious, had a sixth sense about the cops and about the thugs that would rip off dope dealers. He wasn't greedy, and he respected other dealers' territory and customers. He wasn't a big physical type, so he had to use his brains to keep out of harm's way. He had developed regular customer that he got to know. That kept him out of jail because he didn't have to stand on street corners to sell his wares. He delivered to many of his customer's homes.

Carver was the kind of person that he would normally would want to have as a client. There were a couple of things that were bothering Tommie about this broad. After all the time that she had been coming into the bar, now she suddenly develops a habit for dope. And she wants heroin – but she never used it – and she don't know what to do with cocaine. He would have walked away from her if not for the fact that she had the look of a hype. A hype in real bad shape.

"I'll pay you fifty dollars to show me how to use cocaine," Lavern said in a pleading way.

Tommie was thinking. Is this broad for real? Here was this old bitch begging him to show her how to do drugs. Tommie who was in his earlier twenties thought that Lavern being in her late forties or early fifties was an old woman – not a bad looking old woman, but an old woman none the less. The money that she was offering for instructions was not important. All of a sudden Lavern became a curiosity factor for Tommie. This was a new approach. If the cops was using this old broad to set him up then he was a set up dealer. He had to find out what was to this old lady.

"Who you live with?"

"I live by myself."

"Where you live?"

"Not far. Just a few minutes away."

"You driving?"

"Yes."

"What kind of wheels you driving?"

"What?"

"What kind of car you driving?"

"A grey Ford. It's right outside."

"Ok! We'll do it. You wait here for 5 minutes, then go get in your car. I'll be behind you."

"Lean over."

"What?"

"I said lean over. I'm gonna hug you. I'm gonna rub my hands on your back and across your tits to see if you is wired."

Lavern reluctantly complied. Tommie checked her out. She was clean.

Tommie left the bar and got into his car. He could see Lavern exit the bar from where he was parked. She drove off and he followed her. Lavern did not go in the direction that Tommie had expected. She headed toward a section of town that contained some fashionable apartments. Cooks or maids could not afford to live in that section of town. Tommie's interest was further peaked. Although his curiosity had him, he was still thinking caution. Drug dealers had to be cautious. The thought entered his head maybe this old broad in some kind of way - was trying to rip him off. He better leave most of his stuff in the car. She could be some kind of decoy for some dudes waiting in her apartment. That was unlikely but in his business Tommie couldn't afford to not think of any possibility. Thinking had kept him out of jail and free from bodily harm throughout his young drug dealing career. He reached under his seat and put a small pistol in his pocket.

After about five minutes of driving, Lavern pulled into a parking lot next to an apartment complex. Tommie parked next to her. He reached under the seat of his car and pulled out a carrying case that contained his product and drug paraphernalia. Lavern exited her car and waited until Tommie joined her. They proceeded to go to her apartment. They walked to the entrance of the apartment in silence. Tommie looked at Lavern out the corner of his eye to try and detect any change in her demeanor that would give away a trap that lay waiting for him. He detected none that would indicate that there was danger ahead for him. He detected the signs that he had seen in other drug addicts when they needed a fix real bad. Tommie had to help her with her keys at both the building and the apartment door.

Upon entering the apartment, Tommie quickly assessed its condition.

The disarray of her apartment jumped out at him as soon as the door was open. It was another good sign. He knew that a real dope addict was not a neat person. All they cared about was -   where the next fix was going to come from. If her apartment would have been neat, Tommie's fears of a set up would have been heightened. He untensed and relaxed a little.

He pretended to be admiring her quarters as he walked around, telling her, "Mama you got a nice little abode here. Real cute and cozy."

He was really checking her crib out to see if anyone else was there. Her kitchen was visible from the front door through her small living room. Before she could close and lock the front door he had made it to the kitchen door and looked out through the curtains to ensure that no one was waiting on the back porch to bust in on them. He then sat down on the kitchen table and beckoned Lavern who had sat on the living room coach-to join him. She did. Tommie attempted to engage Lavern in some small talk.

He asked her, "what kind of work do you do? I didn't figure that you lived in this part of town. Nobody don't mop no floors and cook no hamburgers and pay rent in this building. So, what's up with you? How do you get your ends together?"

Lavern ignored his questions. She asked him how much was the cocaine that he had told her about.

Tommie replied by throwing out his hands and saying, "Gez, baby you really want to get down to business. Ok! Ok! but look first I got to go to the bathroom."

Tommie hadn't checked out the bathroom and the bedroom. He wasn't going to do any business until he was completely satisfied that he and Lavern were alone in the apartment. Lavern pointed him in the direction of her bathroom and Tommie went. The bathroom and the bedroom could not be seen from the kitchen table. They were opposite one another. On the way to the bath room' Tommie opened the bedroom door and gave it a quick look see. Nothing there but a mess.

Same thing in the bathroom. Tommie urinated and went back to join an anxious and nervous Lavern.

Tommie told Lavern that he could do the whole thing for a hundred bucks. That would cover him showing her how to cook the cain and the price of the cain. Lavern took her purse from under the kitchen table and pulled out a wad of bills.

"Damn baby! You carry that kind of money with you?" Tommie asked in an incredulous way. "You better be careful. Scum bags knock a lady in the head if they knowed you had that kind of money on you," he further admonished her. "You ain't got nothing to cook this shit with? Do you?"

"I don't know. How do you cook it?" asked Lavern.

"That's ok. I'll sell you my works and whatever you need to get you high. Make it a hundred and fifty bucks. That'll cover the cost of everything." Lavern peeled off eight 20 dollar bills. Tommie watched her intently as she counted out the money. He wished that he had quoted her a higher price. She probably would not have squawked about it. Tommie reached into his carrying case and pulled out a glass pipe that was used to cook the cocaine in. Two tin foil packages were also produced. One contained baking soda and the other held an amount of cocaine. A blow type cigarette lighter was the last thing that he pulled from his bag. He began to mix his product while explaining to Lavern the steps that must be taken in order not to waste the substances and to get the best possible effect from the drug. He watched her as he mixed the baking soda with the cocaine and then he lit the concoction. Her eyes were intent on watching the mixture cook. He believed that she wasn't paying any attention to anything that he was saying as he gave instructions to her. It appeared that she just wanted to get to the end product. After a few minutes he was through with the cooking and passed the pipe to her to inhale the brew that would send her on a mellow journey.

She eagerly put the pipe in her lips and inhaled the willowy white smoke that appeared in the bowl of the transparent glass pipe.

"No, no baby don't blow it out," Tommie instructed.

Lavern began to blow the smoke out of her mouth like she was smoking a cigarette.

"Keep it in. Keep it in. Hold your nose…get in in your head… then you get the feeling you looking for," he further instructed.

She did as she was told. After few minutes Tommie could see that the drug was beginning to take effect. Lavern's face began to relax. She had been on pins and needles ever since they met in the bar. The lines seemed to leave her face as the drug began to do its work on her body. She sunk back into the chair and sort of stared straight ahead at Tommie – looking through him.

"First time you ever had the White Girl," Tommie said referring to one of the slang names used for cocaine. "That's some bad shit baby and my shit is known to be good because I don't cut it - much."

Lavern was hardly listening. She was smoking the rest of the pipe and getting a different kind of high than she ever had.

When she had smoked up his first batch, Tommie asked Lavern whether she wanted some more. She nodded that she did. She had used only one dime bag. Tommie was way ahead on the money. He cooked up another quantity for her consumption. She smoked it all. He looked at her and could tell that she was cruising. He tried to make conversation with her, but he knew that she couldn't talk. She was enjoying her high. Talk would have made her to have to concentrate – that would have messed up her euphoria. There was some scotch on the kitchen table. Tommie got a couple of glasses and poured a drink for himself and for Laverne. Tommie did not use drugs. He had seen what they did to his customers. He wouldn't spend his hard-earned money on the shit. Lavern began drinking the whiskey and in no time she was ready to flop out. She laid her head back on her shoulders and slouched down in her chair. She was limp at the table.

Tommie looked at Lavern, sort of satisfied. His product had done the job.

"God dam, oh girl! You in your blue heaven," he told her. "Come on! We going to lay you down before you fall out ah that chair," he continued to talk to her while lifting her on to her feet.

He half carried her, half drug her to her bed room and lied her face down on the bed. Tommie knew that Lavern was going to nod out. He hadn't expected that it would happen so fast. She was new to cocaine and it took her out fast. Her passing out was going to give him an opportunity to find out about this woman. After he put her in the bed, he went to the front door and put the chain in place. He didn't know if she had an old man or someone who had a key, who would enter her apartment while he was there. He didn't want anyone busting in on him. He then began to search her place.

He looked in her dresser drawers and found out what kind of underwear she wore. The cabinets in the bathroom yielded the type of feminine products that she used. The closet shelves gave him a history of her life. Three photo albums produced pictures of Lavern and what he supposed were her family at different stages of her life. He saw two girls whom he surmised to be her children and there were two sets of wedding pictures of Lavern getting married. Tommie wondered where the men in the wedding pictures were. A large envelop on the closet shelves produced her degrees in nursing from the University of Illinois. Her wallet held her Registered Nurse license.

"God Dam! This old biddy is a nurse and she got a master's degree," he proclaimed. "I knew that there was something quality about this old dame," he said as he continued to talk to himself.

Her papers informed him that she was from Chicago and that she had not been in Atlanta that long. Her driver's license told him that she was fifty-two and her bank account told him that she had a lot of money. He counted three hundred and fifty cash dollars that she had in the apartment. She had this amount after she paid him. Tommie not being a greed young man only took another seventy dollars of Lavern's money.

He rummaged through the apartment until he learned everything that he could about Lavern from the papers in her place. He was careful to put everything back as it was. Hoping that she would not discover that he had searched the apartment. He went back to the bed and sat on the edge of the bed and looked at the sleeping woman. He sat looking at her for some time. He wondered how this quality old lady came to be a hype. He thought that she was about the same age as his mother and aunt. He remembered that when he was about fourteen years old, he had delivered groceries to an old lady's house and she had come to the door naked. She had thought that he was her daughter at the door. The woman, although she was old with sagging breast and a pot belly, had aroused him. That thought, sexually aroused him now - as he looked at Lavern sleeping. He had never had a woman the age of Lavern. He had a hard time envisioning a woman the age of his mother engaged in the act of sex. For him there was a mystique about those older women and sexual intercourse. Did an old woman moan and groan? Did they engage in oral sex? As he looked at this woman lying asleep, pictures of the teachers, the crossing guard, the woman who owned the store, his friends' mothers – yes and his mother – flashed into his mind, he couldn't help but notice that his heart was beating faster. He stood up and looked down on Lavern. He placed his hand on her stomach and gently shook her to see if she would awaken. She did not budge but continued in her deep sleep. He unbuttoned her dress and pulled her breasts from her brassier and bent down and kissed them. There was no response from Lavern. He spent further time looking at and feeling her genital area. Now, fully aroused he stood up and straddled her while she lay on the bed. He then mounted her with his clothes still on. It was a passionless act of intercourse that he engaged in. It was an act committed more out of defiance of his mother, teachers and other woman authority figures that he had known in his life. It was not for the pleasure that he partook of Lavern. He wanted to hurry and climax and spill his seed on her stomach. He did. His white substance on her chocolate abdomen freed him from the myth of the purity of older women.

Tommie wiped Lavern off with her panties and covered her up. She continued to sleep. He wondered whether she would know that she had

had sex when she woke up. He hoped that she would. He thought that he should have climaxed inside of her. She would have been sure to know it then. She looked peaceful in her sleep.

"Wow! A registered nurse with all those degrees. How did she turn out to be a hype?" Tommie asked himself -again.

He spent a little more time just sitting and staring at Lavern wondering what brought her to her present situation. He then realized that it was getting late. He had customers to satisfy. He bent over and kissed Lavern goodbye on her forehead. He pulled down the blinds that hung above her kitchen curtains and made sure the apartment was locked as he left. He left her a couple of bags of product on her night stand. The money that he got from her was more than enough to cover the supplies he had had given her.

Four days later Tommie was sitting in that same bar where he had encountered Lavern for his first sale to her. She walked in looking a little haggard. Inwardly, Tommie became a little uneasy when he saw her walk through the door. His deportment remained cool, but he wasn't sure whether she would scream on him for the money he took or to cry rape for her body that he had violated. She saw him and came directly over. She meekly greeted him.

"Hello Tommie," she said.

The tone of her salutation reassured Tommie that she did not have a problem with him.

"Hey lady," he returned the greeting.

Tommie was sitting with two friends. Lavern asked to talk to Tommie alone. He told her to have a sit at the bar and he would be with her. She bought a drink and Tommie, after taking some ribbing from his friends about banging an old broad, joined her. She asked him to sell her some more of his stuff. Tommie told her that he could do that. She also asked him to accompany her home because she was not sure that she had cooked the stuff just right. A little concern entered Tommie's

45

mind when she requested that he go home with her. Maybe someone is waiting to kick my ass for what I did. He thought, but fear or not, Tommie knew that he would accompany Lavern home. For the past few days he had been thinking about her wondering whether he would see her again. He normally sold dope to people, but he did not become involved with customers personal lives. But his escapade with her stimulated a desire to have this old lady again and find out more about her life. Besides he never sold drugs out of the bar. His customers were on house calls.

Yes, he had been thinking about Ms. Carver consistently since he had the encounter with her days ago. She was a mystery to him. How could this nice old lady with her background be into dope like she was. He had sold a lot of dope to a lot of people but to the best of his knowledge he had never sold to such a quality type. Lavern reminded him of his mother. She looked somewhat like her, had a body frame similar to her and even walked like her. Ms. Carver had the kind of job and the degrees that his mother would have liked to have. His mother had middle class values, taste and outlook on life, but she had been poor all of her life. She had exalted Tommie and his brothers and sisters to achieve an education in order to escape the lifestyle that she had to raise them in. None of them had lived up to her expectations. According to her, they were all failures. Tommie, despite his money and the material things that he had, because of his dope trade was the biggest failure of her brood. She knew that he dealt drugs and she scorned him for it. His mother was cold and unapproachable. She had always been that way. He could never show her that he loved her – and he very much loved her and wanted her approval. When he lived at home, he often saw his mother undressed and naked. He had a desire for his mother. He wanted to make love to her. He moved out of his mother's house when his urges for her became too strong.

Anyway, his mother shouldn't castigate him. In his eyes, she was the failure, too. What had she achieved? She raised her six kids dirt poor. She was on public aide. Tommie didn't know his father. Nor did some of his brothers and sisters. His mother could not supply them with a lot of the bare essentials in life, yet she was always telling them about the finer things in life and that they should strive to get them. Maybe if she would have made something out of herself, she would have been able to do more for her kids then just criticize them for not living up to her expectations. He felt that she shouldn't have had children if she could not supply them with the necessary things to achieve what she wanted them to accomplish.

His mother was a Lavern Carver wanna-be. This lady was a nurse and she had degrees, a profession and money. If she wasn't a dope addict, Ms. Carver would be the kind of woman that Tommie would have taken home to show his momma. He would have told her that this is the kind of woman that she should have been. His momma was always pointing out to him successful Black people his age and telling Tommie that he should have been like that person. To his way of thinking, if his momma could have been a successful person he - might have turned out better. He loved his momma, but she ought not put all the blame on him for what he was.

Tommie never wondered or worried about the lives of any other customers. They bought dope from him. He sold it to them and kept stepping. Unless they owed him money, he couldn't care less about what they did. He didn't think about what motivated them to use his product. Ms. Carver was different There was something about this woman that wouldn't let go of him. Why was this woman using dope?

Despite his fear that she might have retribution waiting for him, he again went home with her. They left the bar in separate cars again and arrived at her apartment. Tommie went through the same ritual of checking out the place after they got there. His fears proved to be unfounded. There was no one waiting to bash his head in. He noticed that Lavern had the pipe, baking soda and lighter on the kitchen table, waiting to put them to use. Tommie did not go to the table. He sat on the couch in the living room. He expected her to say something about either the sex or her money – both of which he had taken. Lavern exhibited no interest in talking about either of those subjects. She wanted Tommie to sell her some cocaine and to mix her drugs. She moved from the couch to the kitchen table as if to say to Tommie – let's take care of business. Tommie was determined to talk.

"You Don't seem to be from the south. You talk like a Northerner."

"I was born in the South but I spent most of my life in Chicago."

"Oh yeah! Chi-town. I heard a lot about Chicago. One day I hope to go there. "You think I'll like it?"

"You probably would."

Tommie mixed the drugs as he talked. Well, he thought, she told the truth about where she was from. Tommie already knew a lot about her from going through her belongings. He prolonged the cooking of the drugs in order that he could pry more information from her. He knew that as soon as she started smoking the cocaine she wasn't going to talk any more. He found out how long she had been in Atlanta. She told him that she was a nurse and he also found out that she had resigned her position at Jackson Memorial Hospital. She told him that she had some trouble and that she had to resign in order to protect her license. Tommie resolved there and then that Lavern would be his regular customer. He reasoned that he would not let her fall prey to any other dealer that might abuse and misuse her. He would protect her. The thought never crossed his mind from that point on – or did he let it surface – that his theft of her money and his misuse of her body was his own abuse.

After more disguised interrogation of her in which he increased his knowledge of Lavern, Tommie finished preparing her drug. He joined her in drinking whiskey that was at the kitchen table. He noticed that there were dirty dishes in the sink which indicated that she was eating regularly. She alone inhaled the smoke that would give her the numbing high that she sought. Tommie watched as she went from an anxious state to a relaxed then floating existence. Tommie coolly watched her get high to the point where she would lose her sensibilities. He anticipated having her. He became highly aroused when she laid her head on the table. It was the sign that she was ready to go to sleep. Tommie led her to her bed. He waited for about fifteen minutes to make sure that she was knocked out. Then he completely disrobed her and had her. This time it was not passionless. He kissed her and caressed her and climaxed within her body. He fantasized that he was making love to his mother. After this sexual encounter with Lavern, everyone thereafter was thought of by Tommie as a carnal knowledge affair with his mother. He reasoned that Lavern would wake up wet and know for sure that Tommie had had her. He would discontinue his sexual activity if she protested. She did not.

Before he left her apartment, Tommie got his money from her purse and wrote down her number that he took off of her telephone. He would call her when he had a supply of drugs and tell her that he would come by and bring her drugs as she needed them.

Thereafter, for the next weeks, Tommie regularly came to Lavern's apartment. He made connections with the guy selling heroin and he bought Lavern her drug of choice. His mark up on the drug made him a good deal. He was truly fascinated by her, but he never let his emotions show unless she was high and almost incomprehensible. He developed his own system to find out everything that there was to know about Lavern. He would engage her in conversation probing, here and there, until he found out what he wanted to know. He would withhold her drugs until she filled in the specifics piece of information that Tommie was after. He found out that she had been using drugs stolen from her hospital patients and that she had gotten into trouble with her employers for doing so. He learned that she had two children and that one died. They looked at her photo album and she pointed out family members to him. He became familiar with pictures of her husbands, sisters, brothers, Nina, Theresa and other relatives. The hardest piece of information for him to acquire from her was why she had started using drugs. She lied to him at first- telling him that she was curious to see what they would do to her and that's how she got hooked. He believed her until she slipped up and told him one time that her daughter's death had started her on the road to drug use. After that, he displayed a tenacious ability to pay attention to the details of her story in an effort to prevent Lavern from deceiving him.

He asked her how her other living daughter was. Lavern told him that her daughter was doing just fine. She contradicted that when once she broke down and cried lamenting the fact that she had not had contact with Theresa since she left Chicago. It took him a little time after that, but Tommie was able to discern that Lavern had not been in contact with any family member since she was in Atlanta and that she had run away from home. She let the hatred for her husband slip out and Tommie was on the slip like a cat on a rat.

"Why do you hate him? What did he do to you?" were questions that Tommie bore in with.

When Tommie wanted to know something from Lavern he was as hard as a police Lieutenant grilling a murder suspect. But he had an inducement that the cops didn't have. He had her dope. He would withhold it until she was going up the wall. He would give her some as a reward when he got the information from her that he wanted. She finally told him about the sexual abuse of her children, by her husband. The total picture of Lavern's life became clear for Tommie. He was glad and relieved when the pieces of the puzzle were complete because instinctively he knew that Lavern Carver was a good, smart, intelligent woman and that something tragic would have had to happen to her to turn this lady into a drug addict. Tommie would have liked to get his hands-on Ray as Lavern related how her life turned after she discovered that he had abused her children.

During the next two to three months, Lavern came to completely rely on Tommie. She lived for his daily visits and for what he brought with him. Lavern only left the apartment to go to the bank to withdraw money. Tommie transported her on those occasions. Tommie's interest was not only Lavern's money. He was interested in Lavern. He didn't stop to think why he had such a strong attraction for her. Was he in love with her? If he was, he didn't know it. He just knew that there was something compelling him to mother her, protect her and make love to her when she was almost comatose. He was conscious of the mother substitute thing but to really think of that was beginning to make him feel guilty. Although he made sure that he took enough of her money to pay for product, he was not ripping her off. As a matter of fact, he was losing money from his drug business because he spent so much time with Lavern. Which included cleaning her apartment and doing her grocery shopping. He did everything for her. He cooked and made sure that she ate something. He even made sure that her clothes were clean by taking them to the laundry. Junkies don't care about a lot of things that are important to other people. Lavern was now totally strung out and if it were not for Tommie her only shopping would have been for drugs in the streets.

Tommie's sexual interactions with Lavern did progress to the point that he could fornicate with her while she was awake – barley awake. He would never have her sexually unless she was high on drugs. He no longer waited until she was totally passed out, but she still had to be under the influence before he made a move on her body. He wanted Lavern to know that they were intimate, and he expected her to say something to him about it when she was not high, but she never did. When he had her, her body would relax but she never showed any emotion or displayed any feelings. Tommie had come to derive immense sexual satisfaction from her while she was in the state of being high. But he could not bring himself to be aroused unless her mind was muddled by drugs. That was not Tommie's usual mode of operating with women. He was a good looking, sexually active young man who had been aggressive with young women all of his life since he was sixteen years old. But the love making to this woman, the age of his mother, was conducted in an inhibited, sly, calculating manner. He was like stealing her love and her body.

Tommie was mesmerized by the relationship that he was having with Lavern. He enjoyed taking care of her and dominating her life. He fussed at her and issued orders and instruction that she followed. He even bathed her and kept her clean. As long as he brought her what she needed, she did what he told her to do. Tommie would have wanted the relationship to go on indefinitely as long as the money held out. If it were not for the success of an operation that was conducted by the Atlanta Police Department.

Did anyone conspire to get it done? Or was it just luck? Nobody knows. The 'how' didn't make any difference. The fact was, it did happen. The cops made a big drug bust and it affected most dealers and junkies on the streets of the city. The bust was at a warehouse which contained a shipment of drugs that would have supplied the needs of most of Atlanta's hypes for a month. The cops and the city administration were very proud of the good fortune that came their way in taking a quantity of dope off the street. They got lucky. There was a false alarm at a warehouse and when the fireman responded they found containers of cocaine, heroin and weed that were open and laying around the place Someone speculated that the drug kingpins had been sold out or set up for this bust.

Never the less, how it happened, Tommie was affected by the bust in more ways than one. The dope in that warehouse would have eventually made its way through the chain to Tommie's supplier, then to Tommie. But he like every other street level dope dealer got his supply cut off because of the raid. No one had any product to sell. Tommie's problem was compounded because he didn't have anything to give to Lavern and Lavern turned out to be a very different person when she didn't get her fix.

Tommie had seen and dealt with many hypes who were in bad shape because they couldn't afford to get their fix. They begged and did whatever they thought would get them over to take care of their habit. Tommie sometime - but rarely - extended credit to some of his reliable customers when they were down and out on their luck. Most often though, if they didn't have the money he wouldn't let them ride. Those broke customers would go through all kinds of machinations to try and get what they wanted. Tommie would witness their schemes and behavior, but he didn't have to stay around them any length of time and be a victim of their ploys.

But he had to deal with Lavern's efforts to take care of her need to acquire dope under the prevailing conditions. She became a monster when she couldn't get her narcotic. Instead of the docile, subordinated lady that had enraptured Tommie, she became a frantic, anxious demanding and frightening woman who proved to be unmanageable to Tommie. She refused to accept his explanation as to why he couldn't get her stuff that had made life bearable. By this time, the pain of what happened to her children was no longer the overriding motive behind the use of drugs. Her want, need and thirst for the substances became the paramount reason that she had to have it. She had become hopelessly hooked. Tommie knew that, but he had treated her differently then he would have treated any other junkie. He had bumbled into a relationship with this woman. He was not blind to her addition, but she was providing Tommie with a fantasy experience that prevented him from seeing his potential problem. She became frantic and Tommie became frantic in in an effort to try and find stuff to try and satisfy her cravings. He sought out all the sources that he knew through the city and the surrounding area. His search took him into areas that he was not comfortable in, but he was able to come up with a little junk to satiate her for a while. But the drug drought continued, and he was unable to procure a constant supply. The monkey on Lavern's back had hold of her and she underwent changes that went from violent episodes of throwing objects to sickly sweats. During one of her violent occurrences she hit Tommie in the head with a plate. The plate woke Tommie up to the seriousness of his and her plights. Lavern was sick and needed help. Tommie knew that he was not the person to be able to give it to her. Tommie, all of a sudden, felt the urge to get the hell out of her life.

New heroin or cocaine did not come in consistent supply. He managed to get his hands on some product, but it was not enough to quench Lavern's needs. To say nothing of the need to supply Tommie's business. Tommie could use Lavern's money to offset his business losses. Lavern became sicker and more lethargic. Tommie thought more and more about leaving her where she lay and bugging out. He could do that, couldn't he? It might not be easy. As sick as this woman was and with her seeming inability to do for herself, she could waste away and die. If he left, there was no one to look in on her. He felt that he needed to get her some help. Get her to some kind of rehabilitation program. But he didn't want to have his name associated with anything like that. If she laid up in that apartment and expired there might be some kind of investigation into her death. He wasn't sure how long that drugs stayed in the body, but he was sure that they would find traces of it in her. He had seen too many crime TV shows where they did that kind of thing. Finding traces of drugs in her system – that could trigger an inquiry to find out who she got it from. Plenty of people in the building had seen him with her. They'd find his ass easy.

No, he couldn't just abandon her, but he had to find a way to cut her loose. He needed to find a way to divorce himself from the situation where the outcome would be good for him and for Laverne. Besides, he felt a little guilty about and responsible for this woman. Even if he could he did not want to see her forsaken. He had to find a way. But he had better find it fast, he was beginning to feel trapped.

He thought of calling the fire department and reporting that there was a woman suffering some emergency medical problem. They would come and eventually find that she was suffering from a lack of drugs. Maybe they would take her and maybe they wouldn't. She could end up in jail as a common junkie if he made that call. He didn't have anyone else to call. All her people were outside Atlanta. Her daughter was in St. Louis and …. wait a minute, he thought. The daughter. She didn't know where her mother was. I bet she would like to know where her Momma is. She probably come and get her, he thought.

Tommie was elated with this idea. He jumped from his chair and rushed into the bedroom. Lavern was asleep on the bed. He reached into her pocket book that was on the dresser and withdrew a telephone book that he had seen on other occasions when he had searched her belongs. He remembered seeing Lavern's daughter's number listed in the book. He thumbed through the pages until he found her listed under Jenkins.

"Uh huh! Theresa Jenkins. She lives in St Louis, Missouri," Tommie blurted out.

He copied the number down and left the apartment. He would call from the street. He didn't want to call from the apartment. The daughter might have caller ID. He didn't know whether long distance calls could be identified through caller ID, but he wasn't taking any chances. The daughter might think that his call out of the blue was some kind of scheme to rip her off about her mother.

Tommie went to a store and got plenty of change. He then went to the airport. He was looking for a public phone. The airport is one of the few places that still have public phones. It was 7:30 in the evening in

Atlanta. He didn't know what time it was in St Louis, but he hoped that the broad would be home. He dialed the number. It rang three times before a female voice answered.

"Hello."

"Hey! How you doing? Could I speak to Ms. Theresa Jenkins?"

"This is Ms. Jenkins. How can I help you?"

"Yeah! Well you don't know me. My name is Frankie. I'm calling from Atlanta, Georgia. I know you ain't seen your mother for a little while, but I know where she is. I'm calling to tell you that she is sick, and she needs your help.

There was a pause. Tommie didn't know what to think had happened. Was she still there? Maybe this Theresa didn't want to have anything to do with her momma. Theresa finally replied. She asked all in rapid succession

"You said that you know where my mother is. What's your name? How do you know my mother? You said that you are in Atlanta, Georgia."

Tommie replied by telling her,"Yeah, your mamma been in Atlanta for about two years. She been nursing at a hospital here. She ran away from Chicago and she didn't want no one to know where she was but she sick now, and she need someone to take care of her. She left Chicago because of what happened to you and your sister when you was kids."

Tommie gave her that piece of information so that Theresa would know that he was for real. Tommie could hear someone talking on the other end, but the voice was muffled. She probably was talking to someone telling them about the conversation that she was having. Tommie then heard the sound of another phone being raised off the hook. Theresa's voice then came back on line.

"You said your name is Frankie. I am so glad that you called me. I have been out of my mind for the last two years, worrying about my mother. You said that she is sick. How do you know my mother? Why isn't she in a hospital?"

Tommie answered her. "Yeah, your mother is sick but she ain't gonna die if she gets some help. I can't explain over the phone why she ain't in a hospital, but she needs to go. She needs to have her family put her in. I'm just a friend who is concerned about her. You need to come on down here right away and get her."

Theresa told Tommie to please hold on a minute. Tommie could hear Theresa and a male voice in the background. Theresa was probably talking with her husband who was listening on the other phone. She came back on the line.

"Put my mother on the phone. I want to talk to her," she asked.

Tommie told Theresa that he was not with her mother, but that he would make arrangements to have Theresa talk to Lavern tomorrow if that was what she needed to convince her that he was telling the truth about her mother. He made arrangements to call her at 5:30 PM the next day. He also told Theresa other things about her mother so that she would know that he really knew her mother. He could sense elation and exhilaration in Theresa's voice as he gave her the most concrete information about her mother that she had had in two years. He could tell that Theresa was ready to get on a plane and come to Atlanta that evening. Her husband was in the background being a voice of caution. Tommie was running out of change for the phone. He told Theresa that he would talk to her tomorrow. She wanted to talk longer but Tommie told her that he had to go.

"I'll call you sure tomorrow," he told her and then hung up.

Tommie rushed back to Lavern's apartment to check on her. He had forced her to eat a little something before he left. She had thrown up all over herself. Tommie cleaned her up. He didn't mind this time. He could see his problem being over within a few days. 48 hours if he was lucky. He figured after the phone call tomorrow, Theresa would be on a plane from St Louis to Atlanta to get her momma. But he had to get Lavern straight enough to talk to her daughter tomorrow. Tommie needed to get Lavern enough junk to have her head together when he called the daughter. He had to go out and score some junk for her. Lavern didn't have any money in the house. She had been in such bad shape since the drug drought that he couldn't take her to the bank. He had already began using his own money to buy the little bit that he had got a hold of for her. He had even used his money to buy household goods. He was going to have to use some more of his money because he had to have her coherent enough to talk to her daughter. Damn he was losing money all around. Even with the drought, he would have found a way to make money if it wouldn't been for the fact that he was playing mother hen to this woman.

After he bedded Lavern down, he hit the street in an effort to score some heroin. He knew this white boy who was always holding. He hoped that the boy had some tonight. Tommie went to a hillbilly joint in the suburbs to look up the dealer who he thought was a friend. He found him, but the guy turned out not to be in a friendly mood. He was charging three times the normal price for his heroin. Tommie tried to talk the price down, but his friend was having none of it. Tommie was told to either pay the price or hit the bricks. Everybody was uptight because with so few dealers still in business it was easier for the cops to target the dealers that were left. Mid-level dealers were especially uptight. The dealers didn't want to stand around and haggle. Either you bought at the quoted price or you moved on. There were people in the bar that would give you a little nudge to assist you to get to going. Tommie determined that there was no room for negotiations. He brought at the price that would get him the goods. With his pockets considerably lighter, he headed back to Lavern's place.

When he left to go get drugs, he had told Lavern that he would bring her back a hit. He had hoped that the promise would help her keep her wits until he returned. It did but she was on him the minute he hit the door. Tommie had bought enough to give Lavern one decent fix, but he had planned to use what he had to give her three small fixes between then and the time she would talk to her daughter. She had to be alert enough to be comprehensible to Theresa. He would give her a fix now, one in the morning and the last one shortly before he made the phone call. Naturally, he didn't tell Lavern what was happening. As he prepared the drug, he told her he was able to scrap up a small amount of heroin. She could see that the normal amount was not cooking in the spoon. He tied off Lavern's arm and the looked for the vein that would transport the potion. There came a smile to Lavern's face. That facial expression usually came after the drug was in her vein, but her anticipation was so great that Tommie believed her body was seeping in the smell of the drug before it entered the conduit. After the needle was withdrawn from her vein, she relaxed and laid down. Tommie thought, she'll sleep good for a little while. But he wouldn't get much sleep that night. He had too much to do.

Tommie wanted to remove all evidence of his existence from Lavern's apartment. He had a few clothes and some personal effects there. He cleaned the apartment and took things to his car. He even tried to wipe the apartment clean of his fingerprints. Lavern's family would discover that she was a heroin addict. They might want to find out who was supplying her with the stuff. Although people in the building had seen him with her, they didn't know who he was. He didn't want to make it easy for him to be identified. If the family came, as he anticipated that they would. She wasn't going to die. It would not be a death investigation – if there was any investigation. He did not plan to be there when the daughter came to claim her mother.

The little fix that Tommie gave Lavern held her pretty good that night, but she was up about 8:00AM in the morning, looking for more. Tommie had gotten about two hours of sleep when he heard her moving around. He told her that he had gone out during the night and gotten her another small fix. He also told her that he would give it to her if she would eat some breakfast. He fixed some bacon and eggs. She did eat. After eating he gave her the second shot. She relaxed. Tommie went to the grocery store to buy food to prepare for dinner. Again, he used his money. He would bribe her to eat once more before the last shot. He wanted to time the meal and the shot just before the phone call so that she would be alert enough to talk to Theresa.

The rest of the day seemed to drag on for Tommie. Lavern's fix wore off about 1:30 PM. She began to go through her withdrawal behavior after that. Tommie, with a watchful eye on the clock, did what he could to sooth her. He made love to Lavern one last time - to help kill time. At quarter after four Tommie had the meal prepared for Lavern. She had tried to prod him into fixing the meal earlier, but Tommie knew that she was not interested in eating. He again promised her a fix after she ate. She wanted the fix now. Finally, at about quarter to five Tommie gave her the shot. The three shots that Tommie gave Lavern (from what was a one fix cost) were not equally divided. Tommie saved the smallest portion for last. He wanted Lavern to be just coherent enough to recognize her daughter and to carry on a conversation. He did not want her to be knocked out. He wanted Lavern to be mellow when she talked to her daughter. He wanted her voice recognizable but if her speech was slurred a little and she seemed a little groggy, her daughter would detect that something was wrong and that might make her get her butt here faster. Tommie sat Lavern on the couch and took the phone into the bedroom and dialed the number.

The phone hardly rang once before it was picked up.

"Hello."

"This is Frankie from Atlanta. I called you last night."

"Yes. We were waiting for your call. How is my mother?"

"She's fine…really fine… just a little sick."

"Can I speak to her?"

"Yeah. Sure, but she don't know that you know she is here in Atlanta. She ain't expecting to talk to you. Gimme a minute?"

Tommie took the phone back to the living room couch. Lavern was in a junkie nod. Her head was reared back, mouth wide open and her eyes were half shut and glazed. Tommie shook her and she twitched back into consciousness. Tommie told her that there was a phone call for her.

"I didn't hear it ring," claimed Lavern. "Who would be calling me?" she asked.

Since Lavern had stopped working, the only phone calls that she had gotten were from Tommie. He would call checking on her when he was away from the apartment.

"Who is it?" she again asked Tommie.

"It's Theresa," Tommie replied.

Lavern looked at Tommie as if she was searching her brain for recognition of who was this Theresa. She couldn't recollect any Theresa that she knew in Atlanta. She seemed annoyed, as she put the phone to her ear.

Groggily she said, "Hello. Who's this?"

Theresa must have had instant recognition of her mother's voice. Tommie could her voice jump through the phone as she said, "Mom, this is Theresa."

Lavern seemed to recognize her daughter's voice also but a junkie who has had a fix is not going to get excitable. After a pause and a snort and in a junkies cool manner she said, "Hi Baby! How did you find out where I'm living?"

Tommie intently watched Lavern as she listened to her daughter. Theresa was talking a mile a minute. She was talking so fast that Tommie, even though he was positioned near enough to Lavern to hear couldn't make out what she was saying. Lavern would from time to time say "yeah," "no," or "uh huh."

Theresa must have asked about her health because Lavern said, "I'm fine."

When Theresa asked, "who's Frankie?" Lavern turned to Tommie and repeated Theresa's question.

Tommie took the phone away from Lavern. He had given that fake name the night before to Theresa. Lavern seemed relieved to not have to talk anymore. She wanted to finish enjoying her high. Tommie took the phone back into the bedroom.

"Hi! It's me again," Tommie addressed Theresa.

"Where did my mother go?" Theresa asked.

"She's ok. She wanted to lie down. I told you that's she's sick."

"How do you know my mother? Your voice seems so young," asked Theresa.

Tommie did not want to engage in twenty questions. "Look! I know her, and I am trying to help her out. She ain't got nobody down here to help her out. I'm telling you that she needs your help. Are you coming to her?"

"Yes," answered Theresa. "We'll catch a flight out tomorrow morning. My husband and I will come. Give me the address," she requested.

"What time will your plane leave?" Tommie asked.

"We'll catch a flight out about 8:30 in the morning," said Theresa.

Tommie told her that he didn't need to give her the address because he would meet them at the airport, when her flight came in. They determined that the flight would get into Atlanta about 9:45 AM, Atlanta time. Tommie told her that he would look at flights arriving from St Louis and meet her at the gate. He had no intention of meeting her at the gate. He just wanted to be sure that she would come and that she would take charge of her mother. They terminated the conversation – each saying that they would look forward to the meeting tomorrow.

Tommie was relieved that he had about 15 more hours before his problem of being in charge of a human being was to be over. All he needed to do was to insure that Lavern made it through the night and his self-imposed responsibility would be over. Lavern attempted to talk about the phone call with her daughter, but then more important things took over her being – like the need for a fix. She began her frantic behavior by begging Tommie to get her something. She then took to crying and writhing in pain. Tommie started to leave the house and just let tomorrow happen, but he had tried to never let Lavern suffer and beside he shouldn't let her daughter see Lavern in a junkies' dilemma. He wanted her to be in a state when she was coming down off a high. He would go and get her some dope.

Tommie mixed some sleeping pills into a drink and gave it to Lavern. He was going to head out to see if he could find one last fix for Lavern. He then headed back to the suburbs and the hillbilly bar where he scored the night before. When Lavern was out of his life, he was going to work his butt off. His cash was going to be seriously depleted after this. It took him about 30 minutes for him to drive to his destination. Upon entering the joint the saw his contact and approached him.

"Brother you becoming a regular," said the white dealer as he greeted him with a slap on the hand.

"Not really I just got a customer who needs real bad. Can't wait for this drought to end," Tommie answered as he looked around the place "I came to make the same deal that I made last night," Tommie told his white friend.

"Cool Baby. Let me buy you a drink. I got to get the shit. Be right back," said the white boy.

He told the bartender to give Tommie a drink and he disappeared into the crowd. Tommie didn't like having to wait alone in a hillbilly bar. As far as he could see he was the only Black in the bar. His apprehension level was up. This was one of those line dancing hillbilly bars. It was full of people dressed in cowboy boots and cowboy hats and they were all doing those dances that he had seen them do on television. He wanted to take care of business and get the hell out of there. He looked around and caught a glimpse of his contact talking to a couple of dudes just off a bar that was in the back of the place. He strained his neck to get a better look, but they walked out of view.

About 10 minutes passed before the dude came back.

Tommie asked, "God damn man! What took you so long? Did you have to make the shit?"

"No man, just a little problem came up. We ready to deal now. Let's go out back," he said while putting his hand on Tommie's shoulder in an effort to guide him in the direction that he wanted to him to go.

Tommie's heart dropped to his feet. He felt that this could be a set up. Out back he could expect to get his money took and probably his ass kicked – and no dope for Lavern. He was cursing Lavern in his head as he was being escorted out back. He had never let himself be put in this kind of position to get ripped off because he had always been cautious about where he went, what he did and how he did it. But because of this old broad, who had his head for all of this time he was going to get had. Tommie was sweating bullets as they walked in a short breezeway that led to the back door. The crowd was getting further and further away from them. The White boy was a lot bigger then he, was walking behind him. Tommie stopped before he got to the door and went into his pocket. He pulled out his money and turned to face his escort. He was making a last-ditch effort to avoid going out back.

"Let's do it now," said Tommie.

"I ain't got the stuff on me. It's stashed out back," the white boy told him.

Tommie continued out of the door. He couldn't take this big White boy head on. He hoped that he would have a chance to get away when he got outside.

Once outside, the White boy took the lead. About forty feet from the back door he stopped and turned to face Tommie. They were in a dark area behind the bar up a little incline that led to a road that ran behind the bar. A few cars were parked on that road, but Tommie could not see any other person around.

"Ok man let's do it," said the white boy with enthusiasm. He had a small package in his hand that he pulled from his pocket.

Tommie said, "yeah man," as he reached his sweaty hand into his pocket to again pull out his money.

He pretended not to notice that the guy had lied to him about not having the stuff on him. He remained cool, but he was trying to anticipate where the first lick was going to come from and whether he could take it and make a move to escape. They exchanged the money and the dope. The white boy then put out one of his hands and pointed a finger at Tommie and began lecturing him.

He said, "Look Man it ain't cool for you to keep coming out here. Dudes in there wanted to off you tonight. They figure that a Black guy draw a whole lot of heat out here in the boonies. Especially during this time. Everybody here figure you here for some dope. You ain't here to line dance with no hillbilly broad. I told um that you was straight and that I would give you the word to keep away. You and me done business in the city but it's different out here – especially now. I know that you would look out for me and pull my coat if I came to the city and there was a problem…"

"Yea man. I sure would. Thanks a lot for watching my back. I'm cool. I won't need no more stuff after tonight. I just had this customer that I extended myself for. Hope I didn't cause you no problem," Tommie said with considerable relief coming over his body.

They shook hands and the White boy walked Tommie to his car.

Tommie didn't go straight to Lavern's apartment. First, he had to stop on the highway and relieve himself. He could not remember having to empty his bowels in open air and relieve himself since he was a child. That night would be the one that he would talk about for the rest of his life. He could truly say that he had the crap scared out of him. He also stopped and got a couple of drinks. He hoped that the alcohol that he gave Lavern would keep her cool – but the hell with her. He had to get his own self together.

He finally made it to Lavern's apartment. She was in bad shape. Tommie didn't mess around. His nerves were still shot. He couldn't take any of her shit. He prepared the dope and gave it to her fast. It was enough to make her feel good until he could hand her off to her daughter in the morning. Tommie then laid on the couch to get some rest.

At 6:00 AM he awoke. He checked the apartment one more time to ensure that all that belonged to him had been removed. Lavern was still asleep. He wrote a note which was attached to Lavern's bed room door. He figured that Lavern would still be sleep when her daughter arrived. The note informed Therese that her mother was a heroin addict. Tommie deducted that it would be better for Theresa to know what was wrong with her mother. She might think that she had cancer or something and they might waste time trying to find out what her problem was. Theresa might have a hard time accepting that her mother was a dope fiend. He added this to the note: 'your mother started to take drugs after she found out that you and your sister had been molested by you step-father' He reasoned that that would help Theresa believe that it was possible for her mother to have become a drug user.

He left the apartment at about 7:30 in the morning and headed for the airport. Once there he parked, found, and went to the gate that Teresa's plane would arrive at. He put the key to Lavern's apartment in an envelope with a note addressed to Theresa stating that he was sorry that he could not have met her because something had come up. He wrote down the address of the apartment and drew a crude map which gave directions from the airport to the apartment. He sealed the envelop and gave it to the attendant at the gate with instructions to page Ms. Jenkins when the flight from St. Louis arrived. He then went and had some breakfast and waited until the flight landed. Tommie sat at a gate across the concourse from the gate at which the St. Louis plane arrived. He was in perfect position to see the people debark the plane. He recognized Therese and her husband from their picture in the album when they departed the plane. There was another man and woman with them whom he did not recognize. Theresa answered her page and got the envelop. The group huddled around Theresa while she read the contents of the envelop. They stood around talking for a few minutes and then they decided to follow the instruction in the envelop. They went to a car rental and made arrangements for a car. Tommie shadowed them all the while that they were at the airport.

They picked up their rental car and hit the road. Tommie had given them directions that would put them on the expressway and then on the street to get to Lavern's apartment. Tommie knew a faster way and he took it. He figured that he should beat them to their destination by about fifteen minutes, depending on the traffic on the expressway. It was morning rush hour. He pulled up and parked down the street from the apartment and waited. He waited for about 15 minutes and they still had not come. He began to get nervous. He reproached himself for not following them. Where could they have gone? His map was simple enough to read. Maybe they stopped at a police station. He wanted to leave but he determined to stay until he was sure that Lavern was in good hands. At that minute, he saw the rental car turn slowly onto the street. It was going slow. They were looking for the address. They found it and stopped the car. Tommie saw all four of them get out and walk up to the apartment complex. Tommie let them get into the Garden way of the complex before he started his car. He couldn't see them walking into the apartment entrance from where he was parked. He slowly drove past as they were going into the entrance of Lavern's apartment Tommie felt a tremendous relief at that point. His responsibility was over. The lady was going to be taken care of. He hadn't abandoned her.

As he drove away he wondered how he had gotten involved.

"Man, I must ah been crazy to fall for that shit," he said out loud.

For the next three days, Tommie would ride past the apartment to see if the cars were still there. They were, but on the fourth day as he rode by he saw Theresa with her mother walking to the Lavern's car. The daughter was holding her mother ever so gingerly. The two men assisted her to get into Lavern's car. The other woman who came with them was loading suitcases into the trunk. Lavern was wearing a winter coat. Tommie thought that she must have had withdrawal chills.

"Take good care of her," he whispered as he drove away.

He wanted to get out and say good-bye, but he resisted the urge. He never saw or heard about Lavern again. For the rest of his life, he would wonder what happened to her.

SENIOR LOVE

Sylvia is going on a date. She has been invited to take in a movie. At 76 years old, it is the second date that she has had in the last 50 years. In the week prior to this date, she was invited to dinner and she went to have a meal with a gentleman that she had met at a birthday function hosted by one of her fellow retirees. The gentleman was also in his seventies. Sylvia is a retired teacher who has been retired for the last 10 years. She is also married and has been for the last 50 years. The man who asked for the date picked her up and they drove to the movie theater. After purchasing popcorn and other refreshments, the couple settled into two seats in a sparsely attended movie house. The movie started, and the gentleman put his arm around Sylvia and reached across his body and put his other hand on her thigh. As the movie progressed the gentleman kissed Sylvia on the cheek and moved his hand underneath her dress into her vaginal area. Sylvia had not been sexually aroused in years - but she was now intensely stirred up. She was in unfamiliar territory as far as sex was concerned. She briefly thought that she should tell the man to stop but the feeling was too good to ask him to discontinue what he was doing. It had actually been 20 years since a man had put his hands on her butt, breasts or sexual organ in an effort to arouse her sexually. Her body was tense as she gripped the handle on the seat of the chair. She was torn between relaxing and enjoying what was happening to her and being aware that it was happening in this open forum of the movie theater. Sylvia glanced around and realized that there was no one else in the immediate vicinity of their seats (the man had purposely chosen the location for his purposes). She was just about to relax and enjoy the man's probing into her private area when he stopped.

Paul was the name of the man. Paul withdrew his hand from under Sylvia's dress and he whispered into her ear, "Go to the wash room and remove your panties."

"What?" she asked with a puzzled look on her face.

He reiterated, "Go to the wash room and remove your panties."

Sylvia sat for a moment and looked at him and thought. 'I can't believe that this man just asked me to take off my drawers and in the movies at that'. Her first instinct was to say no and to tell him that she was only here to see the movie, but her heart was still pounding from his hand being under her dress and she realized that she was going down a road that she hadn't traveled in a long time and she wanted to see where this adventure would end. The couple sat for a moment looking at each other, not saying anything to one another. Without any further protestation, Sylvia then got up from her seat and headed to the washroom. As she went to the place that she had been ordered to go, she thought about what was happening to her. She thought that her sexual fires had been permanently extinguished. No man had attempted to have any type of intercourse with her for the last 20 years and all of a sudden this man puts his hands under her dress and she finds out that the sexual fires were not out – they only had been banked. On the way to the washroom she started to turn back a couple of times but her awakened sexuality propelled her forward.

She returned from the washroom to her seat with her panties in her purse. Paul said nothing to her and made no move toward her for a time. Then all of a sudden he turned and lightly kissed her on the check. His hand touched her breast. She wanted his hand under her dress like he had done before. He finally did began probing under her dress through her pubic hairs until he found the opening to run his fingers into her virginal area. It didn't take long for Paul to bring Sylvia to a sexual climax using his finger to apply pressure on the opening to the crevice between her legs.

After the culmination of act, Paul let Sylvia cool down from the exhilaration that she had undergone. It was a good thing that the movie was long because Sylvia had to take time to recover. Paul calmly sat back and watched the movie while Sylvia tried to put her mind and her clothes back in order. She left her panties off. The movie ended and the couple left the theater.

After they got into the car Sylvia asked Paul, "Why didn't you take me to a hotel to do what you did?"

Paul answered, "I wanted to do something to you that I don't think that you ever had happen to you - so that you will always remember our first sexual encounter."

As a result of this movie date encounter, Sylvia and Paul started an intimate relationship.

Sylvia was born and raised in Mississippi in the 1930s. Her home was in a rural area in the Mississippi Delta. The nearest town was 10 miles from her home. It is the part of the State drained by the Mississippi River where the soil is rich from the annual overflow of the river. The family owned 50 acres of land. Her mother was a school teacher and her father was a school principle in the segregated Mississippi school system. Sylvia was the second oldest of nine children that were the product of her parents. Besides teaching school, Sylvia's parents also farmed the land. They grew and picked cotton to supplement their meager income that they earned as educators in the Magnolia State. Sylvia came to value education early in her life which was not the usual for Black kids growing up in the rural Mississippi country. She had her mother and father to thank for that in that they were role models for her and her siblings. Although her parents were educated and had land, they were not rich. But they were better off than most other black people in that time frame and in that area of the country.

Although, both parents were educators in the primary school that Sylvia attended, the parents recognized that the level of education that they provided for their daughter was inadequate. They were able to send Sylvia to a private boarding school for Black children that had been funded by Northern Philanthropists during the country's reconstruction period after the Civil War. Sylvia graduated from that school and then attended one of the all Black Colleges in the State. She matriculated with a major in biology in 1956 - at 20 years of age.

After graduation from college, Sylvia returned to her parents' farm which she had only visited during summer breaks for the last 6 years. When she returned she was not mentally ready to pick cotton or even to teach school in rural Mississippi for the rest of her life. She hadn't been anywhere in the world outside the farm and the schools she attended, but she had adventure in her blood. She was ready to say goodbye to rural Mississippi. Sylvia had an aunt that lived in Chicago and the aunt invited her to come live with her.

Sylvia packed a bag, kissed her parents and sibling goodbye, got some money from her father, hopped on a Greyhound bus and headed for Chicago. Unbeknownst to her, she became a part of the great migration of Black people who left the south for the urban north.

Sylvia arrived in Chicago on the south side and after being awed by Lake Michigan, the museums, the crush of people, trolley cars, the elevated trains and the many bars and taverns in the Black community, she got a job. Her job came just in time because she was about to run out of the funds given to her by her father. Her degree in biology landed her a job as a research assistant in a research facility at an area hospital. The pay was barely enough to pay for her rented room, food and expenses back and forth to work. She sat her sights on climbing the economic ladder for a decent life. The opportunities in Chicago were limited for Black females. There were plenty of jobs for maids, laundresses or housekeepers on the North side of Chicago. Sylvia determined that she did not come to Chicago to be White folk's maid or cook.

Being a teacher in Chicago was more economically rewarding then being a teacher in Mississippi. Sylvia resolved that she would join the teaching profession. She had a degree, but she did not have the courses in education that she needed to qualify for a teaching position with the Chicago Board of Education. She was able to secure a loan to attend classes at night at the University of Chicago to acquire the needed courses that would qualify her to teach and to begin her upward mobility for the kind of life she envisioned. After accumulating the course hours that she needed and receiving the certificate of completion, she applied to teach in the Chicago Public Schools. She was hired and was appointed as a substitute teacher. Normally, substitute teachers are hired as replacements for tenured teachers that are absent. A substitute teacher might move from school to school on any given day. Sylvia was fortunate in that when she was hired she took the place of a tenured teacher who was on a sabbatical leave, therefore, Sylvia got to stay at one school during her time as a sub-teacher. She spent a year as a substitute and was hired as a full-time teacher after that year at the same school.

Before acquiring her teaching position, Sylvia had become involved in a romantic relationship. While working at the hospital, she met a man who was 5 years her senior. Claude Morrow was employed to clean animal cages in the research facility where Sylvia worked. Claude began courting Sylvia. Claude, like Sylvia, was a recent arrival to Chicago. He was from Jamaica. Sylvia was a virgin when the relationship started. About the same time that she became a tenured teacher, she became pregnant. Sylvia and Claude married before the child was born.

At this juncture in her life, Sylvia developed two fixations that would stay with her for the rest of her life. They were advancing education (for herself and anybody that she came in contact with) and helping other people. These qualities first surfaced in her relationship with her husband. When first married, Claude had a couple of college courses. Sylvia was determined that Claude would have a college degree. She pushed him into enrolling at the local Junior college – taking night courses. Sylvia while working as a teacher and taking care of her child (and caring for the second child that came along), helped Claude with his studies. Most every paper that Claude had to produce was written by Sylvia. She continued to assist Claude achieve a higher level of education as he graduated with an Associate of Arts Degree from Junior college. He then successfully completed course work for a Bachelor's and Master's degrees. Without the help of his wife, he could never have achieved his educational accomplishments. Sylvia also did most of the research work and the writing for Claude's Master Degree Thesis.

Upon completion of his degrees, Claude became a citizen and began a teaching career in the Chicago Public School system. With Sylvia and Claude both employed as teachers, their income placed them into the Black middle class. A four-bedroom home was eventually purchased by the couple in an affluent section of segregated Black Chicago. The year was 1968 and yes, Chicago was just as segregated as Mississippi and many other parts of the south when it came to living patterns.

By 1972, the couple had two children and they were enjoying the good life as fueled by their income from their teaching jobs. Besides the home, they had purchased a car and were able to afford to buy most thing that they needed for themselves, the children and the home. But it was about this time that a crack began to develop in the relationship between Sylvia and Claude.

Sylvia's priority was education. She felt less than adequate because she only had a Bachelor's Degree. She envied her colleagues who had Master's and Ph.D. degrees. She felt like a second-class citizen in her academic environment. She tried to take graduate courses on a part time basis but working and taking care of two young children and keeping a house were overwhelming tasks when coupled with trying to go to school. Her outgoing personality was being affected because her level of educational achievement and self-esteem was not up to her own standards. Mind you, most of the teachers whom she worked with also had only Bachelor degrees, but she wanted advanced education. She wanted to feel more valued by her peers and by school administrators. At that moment she was feeling like she was on the educational second string. There is a hierarchy in the field of Education, and those with a Ph.D. are at the top. Her husband had a Master's Degree which she had been instrumental in his acquiring. She was feeling less valued then he and she knew that she had more brain power than her spouse. She determined that she would receive her master's degree at any cost.

After being employed for a number of years in the Chicago School System, a teacher qualifies for a sabbatical leave of absence. In short, a Sabbatical leave allows a teacher to leave the job while they pursue additional education. After the Sabbatical leave is over, the teacher can return to their former position or one like it if the former position had to be filled. Sylvia's years of employment as a teacher had brought her to the point that she now qualified for a sabbatical leave. She applied for the leave and permission was granted to take it. Sylvia had been in discussion about the leave with her husband for some time before the leave was approved. He did not want her to take it because the sabbatical was without pay. The family's income would be cut in half without Sylvia's pay. The combined income of Sylvia and Claude had supported a very good life style - especially for Claude. He liked to dress, and he had bought an extensive wardrobe. Claude took trips back and forth to his native Jamaica during the summer. He liked to brag about his educational credentials and teaching status to his Jamaican family. He was from a poor background and he ego-tripped every time that he went home. Claude also had developed other expensive habits such as dinning in fine restaurants, joining an exclusive chess club, and he had set his sights on purchasing an expensive Cadillac car.

"We can't afford to have you stop working. Without your income we can't meet the expenses to fund what we need for ourselves and the kids," he consistently said to Sylvia.

Sylvia's mind was made up. She put her foot down and told Claude that she was going on sabbatical.

"We will have to cut down on what we buy and if it comes down to it - we will **starve** but I am getting a master's degree" she replied.

So Sylvia was off on her sabbatical. She enrolled at Chicago State University and pursued a Master Degree in Education. She took both day and evening courses to hurry the process along. School was going fine. Pursuing that degree and receiving the grades for the courses that she took was pleasurable exhilaration. But her relationship with her husband was deteriorating. He was having to be more responsible for home and children because of Sylvia's classes and studying. He was not cut out to be a house husband but his gallivanting was being limiting. Sylvia had suspected that he had eyes for another woman or other women. Calls use to come to the house but when Sylvia answered the phone no one would speak on the other end. Before Sylvia started school, Claude was away from home most evenings. Claude would come home from work, eat dinner (prepared by Sylvia) and then he was gone from home until about 2:00AM in the morning. Now, he had to stay home with the children until Sylvia came home from her classes in the evening. Claude was like a caged lion – very tense. As soon as Sylvia came home from classes he was ready to hit the street – and he did.

In due course, Sylvia received her Master's Degree and returned to work. She continued to take classes at the University of Illinois because it was her intension to acquire the Ph.D., and besides her employer paid teachers at a higher rate of pay for courses completed beyond the Master's Degree. Sylvia eventually completed all the courses that she could at the University of Illinois but did not get the Ph.D. because she never formally enrolled in a doctorate program or wrote a dissertation for a doctorate degree.

Sylvia stayed employed with the Chicago Public Schools for a number of years - teaching at the high school level. She remained employed with that employer until she earned enough time to qualify for a pension. Sylvia then applied for and was hired by The City Community Colleges as an associate professor. She eventually was promoted to full professorship.

As mentioned earlier, the couple had two children. A boy and a girl. The girl being the oldest. Sylvia doted on her children. She intended to expose her offspring to all of the aspects of culture that she had not been privy to as a young girl growing up in Mississippi. She planned to develop her children intellectually and morally to exist and compete with the best of America's children.

She paid to have her brood attend private grammar school instead of trusting their primary education to the Chicago Public Schools. By the time her daughter reached high school age, the Chicago school system had built a new high school that had a facility and a curriculum far superior to other schools in the system. Enrollment in the school was theoretically by lottery. Sylvia applied to enroll her daughter in the facility. The child did not make the lottery selection. Sylvia was made aware that politicians and other Chicago big shots had bypassed the lottery system and had their kids enrolled based upon clout. Aggressively, Sylvia went into action. She went to the school principal and threatened to raise all kind of hell if her daughter did not get in. Initially, the principal tried to ignore her triad. Sylvia was persistent in pursuing her complaint. She threatened to go to every community newspaper with her story. The principal finally relented and her daughter, Sondra, got in.

Sylvia equally presented aspects of culture to both of her children. Sondra took dance (ballet) and piano lessons. Charles, the son, took piano lessons and Sylvia kept him and his sister in the library trying to introduce them to classical literature. Charles was not interested in cultural pursuits. He was athletically inclined. If it had a football, baseball or basketball attached to it, he was interested. Against the desires of his mother, he went on to play high school football and run track. He excelled at both sports and he won a scholarship to college after high school. Even though Charles did not follow the path that Sylvia would have him to follow, she knew that her son was solid. She was not worried that he would not succeed in life.

The daughter was a different story. Since birth Sondra exhibited strange behavior. As a toddler, Sylvia learned that Sondra was socially awkward. Baby sitters were hard to keep because Sondra would continually cry when she was out of sight of her mother. The baby was comforted when she could see and feel Sylvia. She played well by herself but had trouble when she had to interact with others as she entered pre-school. Despite the daughter's uneasiness to interact with other children, Sylvia pushed her child into activities that forced her to relate to other children. Ballet, girl scouts, children's theater and children's craft groups were some of the activities that Sylvia involved her daughter in.

As Sondra grew, Sylvia tried to gage the girl's intelligence. She was brilliant at some things. She quickly learned how to play the piano and played it well. She was mostly no good at problem solving. She came to rely on Sylvia to provide her with solution to her everyday problems. Sylvia over indulged her by doing so. Also, Sondra had one problem that stayed with her for all of her life and helped define her personality. Sylvia, as hard as she tried, could not help her solve it. To put it mildly, Sondra was not an attractive baby, girl or woman. Some would say that she was ugly. On top of her being unattractive, she was jet Black. Sylvia and her husband were brown skinned.

"Where did this black baby come from?" Sylvia asked at the birth of the child.

"Must be from recessive genes," answered her husband - who knew a little about biology.

Sondra grew up in an era when Black was supposed to be beautiful in the African American community. But Sylvia recognized that her daughter's blackness, along with her less then attractive looks was a potential handicap. Therefore, Sylvia reasoned that she had to try and give Sondra every advantage that she could. But the cultural circles that Sylvia involved Sondra in were detrimental to her intellectual and self-concept advancement. The group make ups that Sylvia involved Sondra in consisted of, for the most part, pretty little light skin or light brown skin girls who had no problem making Sondra feel self-conscious about her physical appearance. Notwithstanding, Sylvia continued to push her daughter through her teen years and through young adulthood to try and develop her mentally so that the girl could thrive on the merits of her mind not on her looks, which she was deficient in. The ultimate goal was to raise a child that could succeed on her own as an adult.

The results of Sylvia's pushing of her daughter did not accomplish the desired effects that Sylvia had hoped for. Sondra developed multiple personalities. At times she tried to control and lead social situations that she was involved in. Her peers would have none of that. At other times, she would become withdrawn and would hardly participate in the group activities. Sondra became passive-aggressive and sometimes vindictive. On the whole she exhibited an anti-social personality. The only person that she really could get along with was her mother. Sylvia stood staunchly by her daughter and helped her over any hurdle that Sondra encountered in life.

When Sondra rebelled in high school and refused to do her work, Sylvia stepped in and did her homework and wrote her daughter's papers. After graduation from high school, Sylvia enrolled her daughter in one of the prestigious all black colleges in the south. In the four years that Sondra attended college, Sylvia made numerous trips to the school down south in order to keep her enrolled and to help her with her school work. At the time of Sondra's scheduled graduation, she had not completed her final research paper. Sylvia flew to the school and burned midnight oil for a week until Sondra's paper was complete.

Sylvia's generosity extended to others beyond her daughter. As she taught at the college level she came into contact with many African students and she developed an affinity with those students and with Africa in general. She invited students to her house for dinner, which she prepared. At various times she housed Africans at her house until they were able to get on their own two feet – at no cost to them. Sylvia was introduced into African – in America – social societies and she contributed time and money to help further their causes. She traveled to Africa and visited Sierra Leone and Ghana to acquire a first-hand knowledge of African culture. There are a number of Africans in America who owe in part their success to Sylvia's caring and openhandedness.

Over the years Sylvia's husband troubles increased. By the time their children were in college, Sylvia was resigning herself to the fact that her marriage was all but over. Her mate spent the summer months, when he was not teaching, in his native Jamaica – frolicking with his family. During the school year when he was home he paid little attention to his wife, requesting sex very infrequently. She learned that he did in fact have other women and he became more careless about hiding his affairs with those women. Sylvia heard that he had fathered a child by one of his former students. She had made up her mind to ask him to leave and seek a divorce when a life changing event happened.

Upon arriving home after graduation from college, Sondra informed her parents that she was pregnant. Obviously, some male had overlooked her less then attractive looks and focused on her ample body and impregnated her. Sylvia and the dad quizzed Sondra about her pregnancy – trying to focus on who was the father. To their astonishment, they learned that Sondra had no idea who was responsible for her condition. She told them that she had had intercourse with various males and anyone of them could have caused her to be with child. Sylvia did not deal with recriminations. She knew that it was important to prepare herself and her daughter for the child that would be brought into the world. Over the next months, her efforts were focused to that end. She made sure that Sondra had adequate medical care and at the   end of the gestation period a baby boy was born.

Sondra stayed with her mother for two years after the child was born. She got a job teaching in the public schools and against the advice of her mother she acquired her own apartment. Her mother didn't think that she was ready to make that move but Sondra took her child and moved out and embarked on a life of her own. Sylvia was concerned for her grandchild.

At some point – in the next two years – Sondra acquired a live-in boyfriend. The friend did not work, and he had no visible means of support. Sylvia reasoned that every young woman had needs and that this man was fulfilling her daughter's need for companionship. Sylvia reasoned that based on her physical appearance, Sondra would not have a number of suitors to choose from. Sylvia detested her daughter's man. She knew that he was sponging off of Sondra but Sondra was a grown woman in charge of her own destiny and she appeared to be enthralled with this man.

Sylvia stayed out of her daughter's domestic life until one day she received a phone call from Sondra.

"Mommy I need your help," said Sondra over the phone.

"What's the matter?" replied Sylvia.

"I'm hurt," answered Sondra.

"What do you mean you're hurt?" questioned Sylvia.

"Leonard beat me up" Sondra replied.

Sylvia asked no more questions. "I'm coming. I'll be there in a few minutes. Hang up and call the police," she instructed her daughter.

Sylvia was usually calm and collected but on her way to her daughter's apartment she cursed every driver that was going slow enough to impede her progress to get to her baby. Upon arriving at the apartment, her heart sank when she viewed Sondra. Black eyes, busted lip and a bloody nose were the facial damage visible as a result of the beating that Sondra's man gave her. Sondra's child was a frighten mess as he clung to his mother. The police did come, and Sylvia convinced Sondra to swear out a complaint against her man for domestic violence. The cops indicated that a warrant would be put out and he would be arrested when they found him. An ambulance was called, and Sondra accompanied by Sylvia and her child, was taken to the hospital. The medical staff patched Sondra up as best they could and released her to her Momma. Sylvia took Sondra back to her house and put her to bed in her old bedroom. Sylvia took charge of her grandson. When Sondra was well enough to talk she laid another bombshell on her mother. She was pregnant-again.

In the ensuing weeks, Sylvia, her son and Sylvia's husband moved Sondra's belongings out of her apartment and moved Sondra into the family home. When the incident happened, Sondra was early in her pregnancy. Sylvia convinced Sondra to take a leave of absence from her teaching job so that she would heal and the pregnancy would be less stressful. Sondra and her son benefited from her mother's care and being in a stabilized environment. Another baby boy was eventually delivered by Sondra.

Sylvia continued her successful career as a college professor. Her career thrived – not only did she achieve full professorship but she became Department Chairman of the Biology Department. She was elected president of her alumni association of her alma mater and she became involved in numerous professional educational associations. Sylvia also continued to provide assistance to African students and African immigrants in terms of money donations, counseling and she would open her house to them on a temporary bases when they were in need of shelter.

Her high level of energy allowed Sylvia to maintain her professional excellence and to also support Sondra and her children. As the years passed Sondra's behavior became erratic. After delivery of her second son, Sondra and her children stayed in her mother's house for the next few years. During this time, Sondra would disappear for days at a time. She would show up with no explanation of where she had been nor give a reason for her disappearance. Sylvia would ensure that her grandchildren were not neglected when their mother engaged in her neglectful behavior.

Over the ensuing years, Sondra would move in and out of her mother's home. Sometimes taking her children with her and sometimes leaving them in the care of her mother. Finally, she gave up trying to make it on her own and moved back home permanently with her mother. Sylvia was relieved that this happened because now that her grandchildren were under her roof, she took over the primary role of raising them. She nurtured them through high school and college. Ensuring that their education was financed with a combination of her cash and loans.

As the years passed, Sylvia's relationship with her husband was distant to say the least and it continued to deteriorate. He was a womanizer and he had a hard time hiding it. Sylvia's friends, family and associates knew it and his antics were an embarrassment to her. Claude also developed a drinking habit. She resolved in her own mind that she had given herself a divorce. She had considered an actual divorce after her children had become grown but when Sondra's presented her dilemmas, Sylvia reasoned that she needed Claude's income to help raise the grandchildren. The couple stopped having sexual relationships and Sylvia moved to a room off of the basement that she had had constructed. The couple were civil to each other and both contributed to financing the family expenses with no problems. There were few if any contentious moments between the two. Claude was like a boarder in his own house with his wife, daughter and grandchildren. He came and went as he pleased but had very little interaction with the family. Sylvia and Claude's son had graduated from college, got married had a child and he and his family lived in another part of town.

After working in the educational system for 35 plus years, the couple had had successful careers and it became retirement time for both Claude and Sylvia. Sylvia was in her mid-sixties and Claude was in his early seventies when they both decided to hang up their livelihood and live off the pension that they had earned and the money that they had set aside in 401k investment accounts. The money that they would receive monthly from those sources would almost match the salaries that they received while working.

Upon retiring, Claude went to Jamaica, his birth place, at first intending to stay a short time. His visit turned out to be for three months. He returned home to Chicago and informed Sylvia that he would reside in Jamaica for part of the year in that he had invested some money in a business on the island and needed to be there to manage that investment. He worked out an arrangement with Sylvia that would have him still contributing to the household expenses and residing in Chicago three months out of the year. They would still file a joint tax return. Sylvia was agreeable with that arrangement because she and Claude did not have a life together and had not had one for quite some time. With Claude, the son and the grandchildren gone (the youngest grandson was away in college) Sylvia and Sondra were the sole occupiers of the home.

Sondra worked sometimes as a substitute teacher ,but her behavior became more erratic as time passed. She was in constant demand as a substitute teacher because she still had her teacher certification and there was a shortage of certified teachers in the Chicago School System. During the school year, she would get calls to report to various schools but would only report when she felt like it. When she did work she contributed nothing toward household expenses and her mother bought the food and cooked for the both of them. At this point Sondra was in her fifties. Sondra began hording old clothes, books and other objects in her room and when she did leave the house she had a two-wheel cart that she lugged with her that made her appear to be a bag lady. As the two lived alone in the house, Sondra became argumentative with her mother and in just about every subject that surfaced there was controversy. The two would argue about such things as how the drapes should be positioned and the arrangement of the furniture. Sylvia reminded Sondra that it was her house, but Sondra persisted in her attempt to manage the home. Sylvia came to the conclusion that Sondra had mental health problems but could not force Sondra into therapy. Sondra at times would call the police to the house claiming that she heard noises and indicate to the police that she thought that someone was trying to break into the house. She would get into arguments with the police when they arrived at a conclusion that Sondra had no evidence of someone trying to break into the house. The police left the house believing that Sondra had a mental health problem. Sylvia diagnosed Sondra as being schizophrenic and bipolar without the benefit of a professional opinion.

After Claude left for the Island, Sylvia met Paul at one of her professional association affairs. Paul took Sylvia to a dinner and a movie and reintroduced her to sex in the movie theater. Sylvia had abstained from sex with her husband for many years because there was no mutual sexual attraction between the two. Paul and Sylvia had a number of dates after their first encounters and a hot romantic affair materialized. Sylvia had thought that sex had been eliminated from her life but now she could not get enough of Paul's hands on her body and her hands on him. Sylvia would invite Paul to her house and she would lead him into her bedroom where she would initiate the sex act. Both were in their mid-seventies.

Paul was also a retired school teacher and he was also married to a nice little woman his age. They had been married for years and still had a very good loving relationship, but Paul's wife was beyond her sex life and had been so for a number of years. Paul was very much sexually active and had had sex partners since his wife no longer desired or wanted to be involved in any sexual activity. Paul was attracted to Sylvia for a number of reasons. She was relatively attractive for her age and possessed a nice body. There was no fat or flab but her body was solid for her height and weight. Her breast were still perky and her butt was cute with no lumps or bumps. Her stomach had a little pouch, but it could only be seen if she were naked. Sylvia's age was also a turn on for Paul because unlike some other older men Paul was not looking for anyone under 60 years old to have a relationship with. He knew that there were plenty of older woman who still desired and wanted a romantic relationship. Sylvia's financial stability was also an attraction for Paul. Paul was not looking for nor did he need financial support from a woman, but he was not looking to maintain a woman. Paul had no problem with buying presents or gifts for his lady, but he did not want to have to contribute or pay rent for a lady or play the sugar daddy role.

Paul was over Sylvia's house once or twice a week, sometimes eating a meal prepared by Sylvia and sometimes Paul would bring the meal. They usually engaged in conversations covering topics such as politics or current affairs. They then would retire to Sylvia's bedroom where lust would grab hold of them and they would fornicate until they were spent.

Sondra was completely hostile toward Paul. She did not take kindly to her mother's affair. When her mother began to bring Paul into the house, Sondra was cold to her mother's friend and when she discovered that Sylvia was having sex – in the house – she almost went ballistic. She told her mother that she was appalled that Sylvia would violate the sanity of her father's house. She called her mother a whore.

"You are the devil incarnate," she told her mother. She said, "you compromise my peace by bringing this man into *my* house."

She was relentless in her criticism of her mother's behavior. Sondra was not bashful about criticizing and disrespecting Sylvia in font of Paul. She would make some crude remark about Sylvia in front of Paul and then retreat to her room where she led a reclusive existence. Sylvia would ignore Sondra's remarks and order Sondra to her room. She excused Sondra's behavior and told Paul that her daughter was a sick woman. Sylvia was resigned to Sondra's outbursts and would tolerate them as long as they didn't last too long. When Paul came over to the houses, Sylvia's state of mind was to have Paul satisfy her sexual needs notwithstanding Sondra's antics.

Paul was somewhat confused by Sondra's behavior. It appeared to him that Sondra was putting on a show for his benefit when she would come out of her room and engage in her tirades against her mother. She was most always half naked. She would have a towel or a sheet wrapped around her and as a result of her animated jesters, sometimes her butt or her breasts would become half exposed. She had a big butt and large breasts. Paul would wonder whether Sondra was trying to advertise her wares to him as she performed. Was she trying to entice him with her body? Paul never said much to Sylvia about Sondra with the exception that one time he indicated that if he had a daughter like Sondra, he would put her out of the house. Sylvia indicated that she could never do that. She recognized that Sondra was sick and that if she were put out she would have nowhere to go and that Sondra's children would lose contact with her. Paul never talked about Sondra again.

As time went by, Sylvia and Paul continued their erotic relationship. One evening, Paul was over to the house and the couple retired to Sylvia's bedroom to engage in sex. Sylvia assumed a love making position on top of Paul. Paul could see beyond her to the foot of the bed. The bedroom door was past the bed. Paul was not being vigorous in his lovemaking. Sylvia wanted to be on top – so let her do the work. Paul was looking behind Sylvia when all of a sudden he thought that he saw the door to the bedroom move. The door did move. It cracked open a little bit and Paul could see the outline of someone looking in. It was Sondra.

"God damn," Paul said out loud.

Sylvia didn't react to Paul's utterance. She thought that the declaration coming from Paul was an expression of his enjoyment of what she was doing to him.

Paul thought to himself concerning Sondra's voyerrism,"This bitch wants to watch her mother screw."

Paul flipped Sylvia from on top of him to on to her back. He began robustly making love to Sylvia. He was putting on a show for Sondra's benefit. When they were finished, Sylvia had had multiple climaxes. Paul glanced back at the door. It was now shut. Sondra was gone.

"You wore me out" Sylvia told Paul. "What got into you tonight?" Sylvia asked Paul.

Paul did not tell Sylvia about Sondra peeping at them. He told Sylvia that he could not linger tonight as he usually did. They usually cuddled after sex, but Sondra's intrusion did not leave him in the mood to linger tonight. He made some excuse and told Sylvia that he had to hurry home.

It was alright with Sylvia. She said, "I'm beat, and I will probably fall asleep as soon as you leave. You really did a job on me tonight."

Paul dressed, kissed Sylvia and left the bedroom and let himself out of the house. Sondra was nowhere in sight as he left the house.

Sylvia stretched and yawned a couple of times. She laid on her back with her arms outstretched, as she liked to sleep in that position and fell into a deep sleep. During the night she began to dream. She, like many people, had had dreams whereby one experiences anxiety because you are in a situation whereby you can't breathe. Your dream might take you underwater and you are struggling for air. You are gasping and trying to get air into your lungs. A dream such as this might happen because one might sleep in a position whereby their nose is covered by an arm across the face or their head is laying on the pillow with their nose buried in the pillow. When this happens you struggle in your sleep and the struggle will free you of the position that prevented you from breathing.

That was not the case in Sylvia's nightmare. She couldn't get air into her lungs because Sondra was on top of her, straddling her and pressing down on her with a pillow smothering the life out of her. Sylvia kicked and flailed in an effort to get Sondra off of her, but she was no match for her daughter who out-weighted her by twenty pounds and who was full of venom and hate as she wrought violence on the woman who had brought her into the world.

"You Harlot," Sondra kept repeating as she applied more downward pressure on her mother.

Sondra kept the pressure on her mother until Sylvia moved no more. It didn't take too long for Sondra to extinguish the life out of her mother. Sondra hardly broke a sweat. She took the pillow away from her mother's face and ensured herself that her mother was dead. When she was convinced that her mother was dead, she twice backhanded her across the face as she called her vile names. She climbed off of the bed and stood and looked at Sylvia.

"You won't disrespect this house anymore," she said as she departed the room.

Sondra returned to her room and went to sleep leaving Sylvia dead in her bed.

The next morning Sondra woke and fixed breakfast. She took a shower and dressed. After looking into Sylvia's room and finding Sylvia still dead, she called 911 and reported that her mother appeared to be dead. The paramedics and the police came. The paramedics took Sylvia's vital signs and made an attempt to revive her – to no avail. The paramedics noticed that Sylvia had bruises on her face and they told the police that it appeared that Sylvia had some signs of trauma on her body.

The police questioned Sondra and asked her about her mother's last night. Sondra told them that Sylvia's boyfriend was over last night, and they argued and fought as they usually did. Sondra indicated that the argument was particularly loud last night. She told them that she had to turn up the television in her room to drown them out.

"They went on for over an hour fussing and cussing each other. Things finally got quiet and I fell asleep. When her boyfriend left the house, I woke up as he slammed the door," Sondra told the police.

The police asked Sondra for the boyfriend's name.

Sondra indicated that she only knew his first name, "Paul" she said.

But she did know that he belonged to a professional society that her mother also belonged to it. She gave the police the name of the society. The police took Sylvia's body and told Sondra that it appeared that Sylvia might have died under suspicious circumstances and that an autopsy would be performed They also told her that they would locate this Paul and question him.

An autopsy was performed, and it was discovered that Sylvia died because of lack of air to her lungs (asphyxiation). The police Located Paul through the professional society that he belonged to. His Full name was Paul Meadows. They paid a visit to his home and requested that he come to the police station and answer some question concerning Sylvia's death. Paul did not know that Sylvia had died. He had been trying to contact Sylvia for the last 2 days but had been unable to. Learning that Sylvia was dead was a shock to him.

The police told him of Sylvia death, when she had died and what was the cause of death. They asked him had he been with Sylvia on the night of her death. He admitted that he had been with Sylvia on that night. The detectives that interviewed him asked Paul about the stormy relationship that had been reported to them by the victim's daughter and the argument that they had on the night of her death. He vehemently denied that there had been any tempestuous relationship between Sylvia and himself and that there had been no argument on that night. He told the cops that he had a loving relationship with Sylvia. The cops asked him did his wife know about his loving relationship with Sylvia.

"No, she didn't," answered Paul.

Paul indicated to the officers that it was Sylvia and Sondra that had the rocky relationship. The police initially interviewed Paul for about three hours trying to get him to confess that he had caused Sylvia's death. The police let Paul go and continued to investigate Sylvia's death. They brought Sondra in and asked her about Paul's statement indicating that she and her mother had an acrimonious relationship. Sondra denied Paul's accusations.

"My mother and I always had the best of relations," Sondra said to the police.

The police interviewed neighbors and relatives to try and confirm Paul's story concerning trouble between Sylvia and Sondra. No one could attest to any problem that was occurring between the mother and daughter. Sylvia had kept her problem with her daughter to herself, especially since she felt that her illicit affair was the cause of the problems with her daughter. If she told friends and family members of the difficulties that she was having with Sondra, she would have had to expose the affair she was having with Paul.

The police were anxious to put this case in their solved category. Based upon the daughter's statement, and the fact that Paul was the last known person to have been with Sylvia the night that she was killed, Paul was arrested for murder. He got out on bail, hired a lawyer and went to trial for the murder of his lover.

MONEY IS A BEAUTIFUL THING

Louise's work day was ending. She is an adult day care worker who performs her labor in the home of aged seniors who are not totally incapacitated but who no longer can take care of all of their functions of life. These seniors live mainly in their own homes by themselves. Most of them have outlived their spouses. Louise is a worker who cooks, cleans, grocery shops and assist the seniors in performing minor medical and health care functions.

At 54 years old, Louise has been on a downward spiral in terms of her quality of life for the last three years. She is a very depressed lady. Louise's depression is centered around money or the lack of it. Until three years ago, Louise had enough money to fund a comfortable life style. Mind you – she was not rich but for a black woman with no education to speak of and no inheritance she was doing pretty good.

Louise is now a single woman. She had once been married - a long time ago. She had two children who are now grown. A boy and a girl. The boy is in jail on an attempted murder charge and her girl has three children of her own. Her girl is in an abusive relationship. Louise does not see her much because she feels that she would kill her daughter's man if she ever saw him abusing her baby. But the daughter is in love with her abuser – so that's that. Louise needs to stay away.

Louise had her kids at a young age and she married the father of her son. The marriage didn't last long. The husband took up with another woman and left out of her life. Louise slept around after that and got pregnant with her daughter. She wasn't really sure who the father was.

Louise was devoted to her children and was lucky enough to be able to take good care of them. At a young age, Louise got a job with a company that catered airplanes at the airport. When she started with the company, she packaged meals that were put into first class on the planes. She proved to be a steady and reliable worker and over the years she received promotions with the company. Team leader, shift supervisor and floor manager were ranks which she attained. She was ultimately responsible, on the night shift, to see that carts that were placed on the planes that contained liquor, beer and food were cleaned and prepared for service for the next day's flights. Louise's income rose along with her promotions.

Her starting salary was about 11,500 dollars a year when she started with the company in 1978 and by 2001 her base salary was 40,000 dollars per year plus overtime. Louise worked all the overtime that was offered. Her income as a single mom fueled a very good life style for herself and her children. She never finished high school, but he had middle class money. During the years that her children were growing up, she had a very nice apartment, a new car every six years or so, and she was able to get her children everything that they needed. She liked to dress and bought the latest fashions for herself.

The year 2001 was a momentous year for the country and for Louise. That was the year of the 9/11 terror attacks on New York and Washington D C perpetrated by the Arabs using planes. The attacks vastly effected the airline industry. After the attacks, the airline which Louise worked for just about stopped putting food on domestic flights. Peanuts and pop replaced meals for airline travelers. The company that Louise worked for laid off three-fourths of its work force. About a month after the attacks, Louise lost her job. After 23 years she was without a livelihood.

Over the years that Louise worked, she had saved money in the company matching pension plan. She put money in the plan and the company matched her money and the plan accumulated interest. At the time of her lay off, Louise had a payout of $70,000 from the plan. Louise filed for unemployment insurance and she figured that she would be alright with the funds that she had at her disposal. She decided to take a vacation to visit relatives to lessen the stress of losing her job. Her plan was to look for another job when she returned from vacation.

Louise took her vacation to California and stayed about a month. She spent close to $4,000 on that trip. Upon her return to Chicago, she started looking for another job. She did not feel overly pressured because her finances were in good shape. In Louise's mind she should be able to find a job making somewhat near what she had made for the last 23 years. All the supervisory management jobs that she located to apply for required at least a high school diploma and many required a college degree. Louise had neither. After a couple of years looking Louise still could not find a job suitable to her requirements. There were a couple of minimum wage jobs that could have been secured but Louise passed them up because she deemed them beneath the level that she needed to live on.

At the time of losing her job, Louise was living by herself in a two-bedroom apartment in very comfortable apartment complex. Her rent was $900 a month. A car note of $800 was due each month. She had recently bought a new car before her unexpected job lay off and had financing for 7 years. She had 6 years to go before the note was paid off. Her insurance, utilities and other incidentals added another $250 per month to her expenses. She had lived well within her means and had saved money through the matching plan at work. Her total monthly expenses came to approximately $1,850. That translated into a yearly expense of $22,200.

Louise did not work for three years. She looked for work, but when her expectations of not being able to find the job that would allow her to earn at her previous rate of pay did not materialize, she began to become dejected. She became withdrawn and devoid of energy. She stayed home a lot and just existed. All the while her little nest egg was being eaten up at the rate of $21,000 per year. In three years she had spent 63,000 thousand dollars of her savings. She, at last became aware of where her predicament was taking her, and she seriously got out on the job hunt. She landed some jobs with temporary job firms that placed her in factories as a laborer, but they paid minimum wages and the jobs were in fact temporary. Some jobs lasted months and some lasted weeks. These jobs slowed down the rate of depletion of her funds - but not by much.

Five years after the loss of her job, at age 48, she was in serious financial trouble and she still owed 1 year on her car. She needed a steady income but could not catch on anywhere. She heard from a friend that home health care companies were looking for people to train and she contacted one such agency. She was accepted by the agency and given the training to become a home health care worker. The pay was a little above minimum wage, but you worked as long as the client stayed alive. This work also slowed down the rate of her funds exhaustion but the inevitable was happening. She could not maintain her life style. She fell behind in her rent and was eventually evicted from her apartment. She couldn't keep up with her car note and she lost the car too.

Louise, after her eviction, moved in with a younger sister and her family. Her depression started at the point of her eviction. Her feeling of hopelessness and despair were reflected in her appearance of gloom and despondency. She was non-commutative with old friends and family. She couldn't afford a doctor. She had no insurance, nor could she afford to take off and go to one of the public clinics that her sister recommended to treat her depression. She had to keep the little job that she had. Louise had never been a big drinker but at this time, her consumption of alcohol increased. She needed something to dull her pain. Her sister, who was a religious person, kept after her to go to church. During her life, Louise sometimes went to church. She went to church when she had a new outfit and wanted to show it off. She wasn't into God all that much, but after constant prodding by her little sister, Louise decided to go to church just to shut her sibling up.

Louise picked a church that she had somewhat been familiar with in the past. The church was Catholic. She had been to other churches, but she figured if she was going to a church she wanted to go someplace where the services are short and the atmosphere is a bit impersonal. There was a Catholic church not far from where she was living. On the Sunday after she promised her sister that she would go, she went. Her plan was to have a quiet hour at the church and go back home.

She entered the church and slid into a pew. There were not many other people in the church. The priest came out and started the mass. Just after the services had started, a woman entered the pew in front of her. Louise noticed that the woman was impeccably dressed. Louise thought of herself in her heyday. She used to be dressed like that.

Today, Louise had on an outfit that was not too shabby, but it was old. As the lady in front of her sat down, she nodded a hello to Louise, Louise nodded back. Louise began focusing on this woman in front of her with the confident body language. To Louise, the woman appeared to be in her fifties about the same age as her. The lady was light skinned, full bodied about 5 feet 7 inches tall with beautifully coiffure hair (it could have been a wig). The woman was attractive and oozed confidence in her looks. When the mass was over, both Louise and the woman exited their pews and departed the church. Once outside the woman spun and introduced herself to Louise.

"Hi, I'm Dora" she said.

Louise countered by identifying herself and complimenting Dora on her outfit.

"Thank you," replied Dora.

The ladies then engaged in small talk. Dora asking if Louise came to church often and Louise replying that she had not been to church in quite some time. Dora exclaiming to Louise that she should come more often.

"It will do your soul some good," she stated with authority.

Louise answered, "yeah, I think I will."

The ladies then went their separate ways.

Louise felt good after church. It was the first time in a long time that her mind was unburdened for – a couple of hours – by her predicament in life. She wasn't able to go to church the next week because she had to work with her client on that Sunday morning. She did go the next week. When she got to the church, the woman whom she had talked with briefly before, Dora, was already there. Louise took a seat beside her and the two silently acknowledged each other. After mass, the two engaged in conversation outside the church. Louise didn't intend to but before she knew it she was unburdening herself to this stranger about her troubles and the way her life had turned upside down. Dora was a good listener. She let Louise get it off of her chest. Dora didn't offer much information about herself because Louise didn't stop talking. Dora did share with Louise that her "old man" – as she called him – was serving time in prison for some kind of fraud. She also mentioned that she had a couple of sisters.

On Sundays that Louise did not have to care for her home health care client, Dora and Louise continued to meet at church. One Sunday Dora invited Louise to have breakfast with her after church. The tab was on Dora. Louise accepted. She hadn't been out to a sit-down restaurant in a long time – she couldn't afford it. Dora led Louise to her parked Lexus and they drove to a swanky eatery in an affluent part of the city. Louise kept her curiosity to herself, but she wondered how Dora was able to afford the Lexus and all of the nice new clothes that she had seen Dora wear. She knew that Dora didn't work. During their conversation at breakfast, Dora told Louise that she had tickets to a concert that featured a number of old Motown greats. She asked Dora to accompany her to the concert because she had no one else to go with. The singing group, The Temptations and the crooner Smokey Robinson were headlining the show. The show was more than two months away, so Dora told Louise that she hoped that she would have enough time to arrange to be off on the Saturday night of the concert.

Louise quickly accepted the invitation and indicated, "come hell or high water I'll make it."

After breakfast they walked to Dora's car and Dora gave Louise a hug, a kiss on the cheek and a pat on her back before she drove her home.

"I'm glad we met, and I hope that we will be friends for a long time," said Dora as Louise exited the car in front of her house.

"Me too," replied Louise.

Louise was improving her persona and it was because of her relationship with her new-found friendship with Dora. In between the first breakfast and the concert, the two met at church a number of times when Louise could attend Sunday mass. Dora took Louise to breakfast on those occasions. Louise looked forward to being with her new friend. She was mildly perturbed when work prevented her from seeing her new acquaintance. On one of the occasions – after church, and on their way to breakfast – Dora indicated that she had to stop by her apartment. She had to get some cash to pay for the breakfast. Louise offered to pay for the meal (although she couldn't afford it). Dora dismissed her offer and said.

"No, no. You know that this is my treat. Come on up and freshen up. We won't be but a minute."

Louise accepted the offer and followed Dora into her third-floor apartment which was in a three-story building in a very nice part of town. Louise once lived in this neighborhood before she lost her airport job.

"Damn! this is very nice," exclaimed Louise as she entered Dora's apartment.

Louise was struck by the spaciousness, the neatness, the décor, the cleanliness of Dora's apartment. The floors looked clean enough to eat off of and the furniture was either brand new or rarely used. Louise sensed that Dora knew that she was impressed by her living quarters. Louise also thought that Dora brought her here just to impress her – well it worked. Louise was impressed. They didn't stay long. They both freshened up and left for breakfast.

From time to time, Louise did wonder why she had related so well and so fast to Dora. It had been a long time since she had been drawn to anybody. Maybe it was because nothing had happened in her life for so long. Also, maybe it was because Dora picked up the bill for everything.

The time for the concert finally came. Excitedly, Louise put together an outfit that was old but she looked good in it. In her fifties, she was short (5 ft 3 in) and still petite (size 6) with a big round behind with no lumps and bumps. She had large breasts for a small woman her size.

She didn't wear wigs because her hair was thick and long. Hair is one of the keys to good looks, Louise could style her hair to look 10 years younger than she was. In recent years, Louise didn't care much how she looked because of her depression. But on this day, she wanted to look good – and she did.

Dora had arranged to pick her up and at the appointed time she came. Dora indicated that they had plenty of time.

"We can stop and have a drink at this little place that I know. It is close to the venue," said Dora.

They parked the car and had a couple of drinks at this quaint little bar that was full with concert goers. The concert site was within walking distance from the bar. Louise was excited to be among the smartly dressed crowd going to the show. She hadn't felt this exhilarated in some time. When they got to the concert hall, there were concession stands selling souvenirs and drinks. Before the show started Dora bought Louise another drink.

"Come on girl loosen up. We are going to have a good time tonight," Dora told Louise as she paid for the drink.

The show was great. The entertainers rocked the crowd. They performed many of the old hits that that had been popular years ago. Louise and Dora found themselves dancing in the aisles as did many other concert goers. At intermission, they hit the lobby and Dora paid for more drinks. By the time the second half of the show started Louise was feeling really good. At that point, she was under control, but the alcohol was slowly making her lose any inhibition. She bumped and grinded in the isle as the band played some old time favorite slow jams. Dora was cool. She hadn't drunk as much as Louise.

She told Louise, "enjoy yourself. I've got to drive."

After the show they again stopped at the little bar on the way back to the car. Dora bought Louise a night cap.

"Look," said Dora, "why don't you spend the night at my crib. I don't feel like driving you way cross town tonight. I'll get you home in the morning."

"Ok," said Louise. "I wanna sleep in that big fine bed you got anyway."

As they left the bar to go to the car. Louise began to stumble. She was drunk. Dora had to help her into the car and up the steps when they arrived at Dora's' apartment.

Dora took Louise into the bed room and helped her undress. She stripped Louise down to her panties and bra. Then she took off Louise's bra and cupped her breast with one hand and her behind with the other. She kissed Louise on the forehead, then closed her arms around her and softly pressed her lips against Louise's lips. Louise didn't resist. She was too drunk to resist and then her body went warm as a reaction to Dora's hands, lips and mouth all over her body. Dora laid Louise down and began aggressively kissing her between the legs. Dora reached for and got a dildo out of the night stand which she alternately used on herself and on Louise until they both achieved sexual gratification. Louise was out of it after that. She sank into a deep drunken sleep.

The next morning, Louise woke up with the pain in the head that drinkers usually get when they have overindulged the night before. At first, she had to get her bearings because she couldn't focus on where she was. She looked and saw Dora lying beside her and wondered why she and Dora were both naked. She had to use the bathroom, so she stumbled out of bed and went on a bathroom search. She found it. She sat on the toilet and tried to focus on what she was doing and where she was. Slowly, the connection with her being where she was and what happened the night before correlated. She remembered seeing the dildo on the night stand when she got out of bed and then she remembered what Dora had done to her. She almost got sober when it all sunk in but the pounding in her head didn't allow her to escape the maladies of too much drinking. She got up and went back to the bedroom and noticed a clock. It was 11:00AM.

"Wow," she exclaimed.

She never slept that late. She began looking for her clothes and saw that her panties and bra were draped across a chair. She put them on and looked for the rest of her clothes.

"Dora," she called attempting to wake Dora up.

Dora did not move. Louise went to the bed and shook Dora, but she still did not respond. Louise looked around the room. Still looking for her clothes. She saw a door that appeared to be a closet and she went and opened the door. Her clothes were on a hanger, hanging on the inside of the door. She began dressing and spotted her shoes on the floor of the closet. She reached down to get her shoes when she spotted a valise that was open. There was something in the valise that looked familiar. Louise bent down and then got on her knees. The valise was full of money. She lightly ran her hand over the bills in the valise. There was an enormous amount of twenty-dollar bills. Louise looked out of the closet to the bed where Dora lay. Dora was still motionless. Louise's hangover disappeared. Her heart beat fast. She stuffed four twenty-dollar bills into her panties and closed the top of the valise.

She came out of the closet fully dressed and sat on the bed next to Dora. She wanted to wake Dora up so that Dora could take her home. She began calling and shaking Dora to arouse her from her sleep. Dora did not move, nor did she moan or groan. Louise began vigorously shaking Dora, but her body was limp, and it was cold to the touch. Louise being a health care worker took Dora's wrist and felt for a pulse. There was no pulse. She checked for a breath. There was no breath. Dora was dead. Louise jumped from the bed when she realized that Dora had passed. She began pacing the bedroom wondering what she should do. She needed to call 911. She thought that Dora must have had a heart attack or something. She went back to Dora's bed a couple of times to check Dora again. Louise had seen death before. A few of her senior home health care clients had passed on her. When she was sure of Dora's condition, her mind shifted to the money in the closet. She might as well check it out. Louise went to the closet and pulled the valise to the middle of the floor in the bedroom She opened the bag and began examining the money in it.

"God damn there must be thousands of dollars in here," she said out loud.

She glanced to the bed where Dora's body lay to assure herself that Dora wasn't looking at her – Dora was still dead.

"Serves her right for raping me last night," said Louise.

Louise then made up her mind -she was taking this money.

Louise quickly devised a plan. She would take the valise and the money to her house. She would use Dora's car to transport the money and then come back and call 911 and report Dora's death.

Louise zipped up the valise, put her coat on, located Dora's keys and left the apartment with the money in the case. She drove to her sister's house where she was staying. She took the valise into her bedroom and put it under her bed. She then drove back to Dora's apartment entered it and removed the dildo from the night stand and called 911.

The paramedics came and performed the routine procedures that they try when trying to revive a patient – to no avail. They asked Louise questions concerning Dora and what she knew about the last incidents of Dora's life. Louise told them they had attended a concert the night before and that Louise had spent the night. She related to them that she had found Dora as she was – this morning. The paramedics packed Dora up and transported her to the hospital where she was pronounced dead. The police had been notified of a death and Louise had to undergo some routine death investigation questions. The police were trying to find out next of kin notification information. Louise couldn't help them much. She only knew about Dora's 'old man' because Dora had told her that he was in jail. She also related the information on the two sisters that Dora had talked about. The other tenants in the building didn't know anything about Dora. The cops told Louise that they would be in touch after the autopsy that would be performed.

They took Louise's information and let her go.

After that part of the ordeal was over, Louise couldn't wait to get home. She took a cab and with an elevated blood pressure she raced into her room. She hadn't eaten anything all day, but her hunger didn't bother her so much. She was anxious to get to the money under her bed to count how much was in that case. After she locked her bedroom door, she began counting and grouped twenty-dollar bills into piles of $1000. When she was finished she had 43 piles. Forty-three thousand, six hundred dollars was the total amount. When she finished she peeped out of her bedroom door to reassure herself that no one had seen her with the money. She was feeling kind of paranoid. She sat on the bed in a stupor trying to think about what she should do with the money and how she could protect it. She came out of her trance and put the money back into the valise because her sister's kids might want to pop into her room to visit her as they often did. She decided that she would not be conspicuous with the money, but she would keep it under the bed and spend it a little at a time to augment her meager income.

In days that followed, she learned that the autopsy results confirmed what she had originally suspected – Dora had had a massive heart attack, which had killed her. The police did find and notify Dora's family and funeral arrangement were made. Louise attended the funeral. Dora had a couple of sisters and a mother whom Louise met. They talked about Louise's discovery of the body. Louise expressed her condolence and left the church were the services were conducted. She did not go to the grave site. The family obviously didn't know about the money because there was no mention of it when they talked at the funeral.

In the ensuing weeks and months Louise continued with her mundane life but now her attitude was great. The depression that had been brought about because she lacked money was gone - she now had money. She wasn't being a spendthrift, on the contrary she was being frugal with that money. It was just comforting to know that she had the money. From time to time, she would spend a little to buy groceries, play the lotto or to take in a movie. She even put a thousand dollars in the bank. She intended to put more of the money in the bank. It was her intension to have that money last a long, long time.

One day two plain clothes gentlemen accompanied by two uniformed police officers rang Louise's sister's door bell. They asked if Louise Baker lived there.

The sister answered, "Louise does live here, and I am her sister. What do you want?"

The men produced badges and identified themselves. They were U.S Secret Service agents and that they had a warrant for Louise's arrest. The sister was flabbergasted. She called out to Louise who was home at the time. Louise came out of her room and the two agents placed her under arrest. The charge was for passing counterfeit money. The secret service agents besides protecting the president also investigate and prosecute counterfeiters. The officers had a search warrant. They searched the house and found Louise's stash under her bed. Louise was taken into custody.

Louise had to come clean on how she came into possession of the counterfeit money. It took a long time before the authorities became convinced that she was not in collaboration with Dora and her "old man" who was a counterfeiter and a drug dealer. Dora had money because her "old man" had left her laundered money before he went into the joint. That money was in Dora's bank account. The bogus money was in Dora's closet. It was to be used rarely if ever by Dora. That money was intended to be saved until her "old man" got out of jail. He knew how to pass the bills safely.

Louise was formally charged with passing the bad paper. Louise spent about a year in jail before she was paroled. Her life was destroyed but her little sister, who was the religious person, took her back in and prayed for her redemption. Her path to redemption was now harder than it ever was because she now was a convicted felon. Her depression returned and thoughts of taking her life swam in her head.

SANOMI''S ESCAPE

Sanomi was engaged in the art of dressing and decorating her body. Today she has been longer at the task then was her normal custom when preparing for work. She had to look her absolute best at work this evening. She also had to have a different look then she normally had. It was her last day of toil in a place, in a job that she had dreaded for the last seven years.

All the accoutrements in the war against age interfering with the beauty of a woman were laid out on her dressing table. Oils, pan cake makeup, rouge, lip gloss, eye shadow and liners were being used by Sanomi to achieve an appearance that at one time she naturally had. At thirty-nine years old, her natural beauty had slipped – just a little. A very good-looking woman, she still was. But now, each year, she needed more help to retain her attractive features – and she had a lot of those. At five-foot two, she had a caramel complexion, weighted 155 pounds and most of her weight was distributed to her breast and buttocks. Her thighs and legs were such quality that she rarely wore any dress that fell below the knees and pant outfits accentuated her legs, thighs and behind to the extent that men felt a deep thud in the pit of their loins when they saw her in pant apparel. Those attributes and a thirty-seven-inch chest had been her shinning glory since she was a teenager. Her face was attractive, despite her wide mouth and thick lips. It was a suave sexy face and it matched her friendly, cool, seductive personality. She now weighted fifteen pounds more than when she was at her best, but she still had the kind of frame that made every man who saw her want her.

She knew that she was as desirable as ever because she now had maturity to go along with her erotic and sensual persona. But now, she had to hide the lines in her face and the pudginess under her eyes with cosmetics. She could see the beginning of a double chin that had not been noticed six months prior. The makeup, in just the right amount, disguised the unwanted facial feature – or so she thought. A bulge in her stomach and some excess fat on her behind were being camouflaged by a panty body briefer. Her once firm curves were no longer firm. She could still wear strapless dresses that bared her arms and upper torso, but the flabbiness of her arm muscles was apparent to her. She realized that the flab was starting to appear in many areas of her body. Sanomi reasoned that it was only a matter of time before excess flesh took over. She also knew that it was inevitable and knew how it would look, because her mother and sisters had all succumbed to the fat that will take over many a Black woman's body whether they are careful or not. All the women in Sanomi's family were fat. Sanomi was now considered to be voluptuous and fine by every man that had the pleasure to look at her, but she knew that she was destined to be overweight.

The knowledge that she would be portly did not now worry her. She had won her race against time. She would no longer have to be a sex object that she had been all of her life. This evening, when she went to work to quit her job, it would be the beginning of a new life. She had planned for this new life for the past 10 years and it was now coming to fruition. She determined that, after this evening, it wouldn't matter if a man ever looked at her again in life. Well, maybe if she found the right guy, it could be ok, but a man would never again dominate her life.

As she continued to dress for work, she finished with the makeup portion of her task. She then turned her attention to the outfit that she had chosen for this occasion. She was careful to pick and purchase a special attire for the last day on the job. What she would wear today, would be different from what she usually wore to work. She had picked a business suit, light gray in color, with a turtle neck sweater to wear for her finale. She made sure that the suit that was purchased was loose fitting, that the length of skirt fell below the knees and that nothing was exposed. When she walked into work, that outfit was sure to grab the attention of everyone in the establishment because no one had ever seen Sanomi in such conservative attire. Sanomi was going to change her image. She might as well start tonight. All the outfits that she normally wore to work thrust out and exposed (to the legal limit) her buxom breasts and accentuated the protuberance of her behind. Those outfits worn by Sanomi were legend and they were part of the success and the attraction of Sanomi and the place where she worked.

Sanomi was and had been for the last seven years the night barmaid and manager at Winston's Lounge on the South Side of Chicago

As Sanomi dressed, she glanced at her watch and determined that she would be late if she did not hurry. She had been so engaged in thoughts of her anticipated escape and victory that she had blocked out the noise of her five children and grand babies They were making their usual commotion in the apartment on the other side of her closed bedroom door. It was the noise that her family made at that time of the evening when her oldest daughter was trying to gather her siblings to feed them. Sanomi had four girls and one boy. The oldest was twenty-two. The youngest, who was the boy, was fifteen. All of her children lived with her. She had all of them by the time that she twenty-two. Her children had been fathered by three different men. None of those men were now in her life nor had they been for some time. Sanomi had no idea where they were nor did she care. She had learned to struggle, quite successfully, to raise her brood without them. She had done a lot of things in her life that some others might be ashamed of, but she had no qualms about what she had done to keep her family well fed, housed and clothed. The important thing was that she had been able to have the money that she needed to keep her family intact with a combination of money received from public aid, jobs in bars and men.

She threw open her bedroom door and began barking orders to her kids as she applied the finishing touches to her dressing. The orders were the same that she gave every day as she left for work.

"I don't want to come home and find no dishes in the sink," she told her second oldest daughter.

The youngest daughter who was eighteen and still in high school was instructed to do her homework. She ordered the youngest, the fifteen-year-old son, to be in the house before ten o'clock. She knew that he wouldn't obey. He had become stuck on a little neighborhood girl that he was spending a lot of time with. She needed to supervise him more closely at this crucial age. She rationalized that it was better to temporarily lose him to the little girl then to the street gangs. Sanomi knew that the street gangs were recruiting. Her son's interest, at the time was for the opposite sex – not the street gangs. She hoped that he would not get the little girl pregnant, but she could recover him from the little girl – maybe not from the gangs. She needed a little more time and then she would have her life in order and she could provide him with other alternatives.

She had been somewhat lucky with her girls. The three oldest had all made it out of high school despite the fact that two of them had their own babies and were on public aide. The youngest girl was a senior about to graduate. Her oldest daughter, didn't have any babies but she had been into drugs and had made a successful trip to rehab. She was back home now and trying to get her life together. Sanomi felt responsible for her problems because she had relied on the girl, too much to care for the family. Sanomi had put her in charge of her siblings while Sanomi did what she had to do to finance the home.

Her glance at the hallway clock spurred her on to leave for work. She kissed her grandbabies goodbye and rushed out of the house. On the street, she slid into a Cadillac that had been given to her (used) by Harold Winston, the owner of Winston's Lounge. It was in great condition. Sanomi thought that it was good that the car was in her name because Harold would probably want to take it back before the evening was over.

As she drove to work, Sanomi thought about the things that had happened in her life that brought her to this day. By the time that she discovered that men would use false pretenses to be with her, she was twenty-two and had five babies. Before that, men told her that they loved her, and she believed them. Then they left her high and dry and went on to other women. They couldn't handle or afford the responsibility of babies. She had only public aide to depend on. She began going to the bars with a girlfriend and discovered that men would get into a bidding war for her favors. They would pay her bills, take her grocery shopping, help support her family and do other financial things for her. She no longer fell for the 'I love you' exaltation. Love was money. She learned that the men best suited for her were older and married She could string two to three of them along at the same time. If one found out about her other relationships and wanted to put her down – that was fine. She could always find another to take his place. Her multiple relationships rarely got her into trouble. She did get slapped around a couple of times when one sugar daddy would find out about another, but Sanomi accepted the risk of violence from men. She began working at bars, as a barmaid. It was a good job for her because the owners would pay her in cash. She could hide those earnings from public aide and thus remain on the dole. She could also select from a vast pool of potential sponsors (men) who would contend for her affections.

After she had been working in the bars for about three years, she met this guy who was a professor at a community college. Many professionals came into the bars where she worked. The professor would tell her that she had a good head on her shoulder and that she ought to go back to school. Sanomi hadn't finished high school but she realized that she did not want to make her living the way she was making it forever. It bothered her for her children to have to see different men exit her bedroom. The professor helped her get her GED and she enrolled in his classes at the local community college where he taught. He taught English and she enrolled in his classes and got a start (with his help) on getting a college education. Her jobs, that she had as a barmaid were in the evening, so she was able to take two courses every semester during the day. In four years, she graduated from community college and then enrolled at a four-year college as a junior. Many women teachers drank and socialized at the bars where she worked. They became her role models. They had their own money and they were respected. Sanomi aspired to be a respected woman. She could have respectability as a teacher.

Sanomi met Harold Winston after he had come into some money as a result of an auto accident. He was a cab driver. He used that insurance settlement money to purchase a lounge. Harold hired Sanomi as his manager and night barmaid. Her personality and business acumen turned the place into a success. Harold demanded that Sanomi be his woman, despite the fact that he was married. It was against her better judgment to go with her boss, but he persisted. Sanomi recognized the potential of being in control of Harold and she relented. Between her salary, what Harold gave her, public aide, what she appropriated from the bar and romancing other men, Sanomi made out all right.

Harold turned out to be a fool. He was jealous, a womanizer and a drunk. If it wasn't for Sanomi's management of the bar he would have lost the business. Over the years, Sanomi found it hard to put up with the boss's antics. He began to disrespect her by sexually having women in his office and if he got drunk enough he would abuse her after closing time by forcing her to have sex in a booth. But as the years passed, she got closer to achieving the goal of leaving the street life. She endured Harold's disrespect and degrading behavior toward her. She knew that she was in control of her destiny.

Sanomi pulled up in front of the bar, parked and went in.

One customers asked, "whose funeral you been to?"

They had never seen her in modest dress before. She greeted them and went straight to Harold's office. Good she thought – he was sober. She informed Harold that this would be her last night. He couldn't comprehend what she was saying.

"What did you say?" he asked.

She told him that that she was starting her last semester and that student teaching would not leave any time to work. He took the news like he really didn't believe it. She started telling him the important things that he would need to know about his business. He asked her what would she do for money. She told him that she would be alright. Sanomi had stashed away enough of Harold's money to make it until she would start her teaching job.

As the evening wore on, reality of Sanomi's leaving began to sink in on Harold. He got drunk and began using insulting and degrading language as he referred to her in conversations with his customers. He got worse as the hour passed. He was embarrassing Sanomi and the patrons.

"Bitch can't steal my money and leave me," was one of the statements he made out loud to no one in particular.

The statements shocked Sanomi. Did Harold know that she was ripping him off – big time? He had never accused her of stealing. She started to leave right then but she had short rung the cash register and had not had the opportunity to take her evenings pilfering from the draw. Harold went to the office and he seemed to cool down.

Later, Sanomi was enjoying herself and basking in the glow of the congratulations from the patrons. They had brought her drinks and were giving toasts to her accomplishments. She did not see Harold come out of the office and walk down the bar toward her. As he approached her, there was a popping sound. The nearest customer to her remembered having her vision blurred by some substance flying on her glasses. The substance was the blood of Sanomi which came from her head as a bullet entered it from the gun shot by Harold Winston. He shot three more times and each bullet entered Sanomi's body at a different place as she fell to the floor. Harold was subdued by the customers and they attempted to administer to Sanomi. Remarkably, she did not instantly die. She hung on for a while and in her delirium, she invited her customers to her graduation.

"Bring me some pretty flowers," she ordered and then passed away.

Sanomi's obituary praised her struggles to better her life and the preacher challenged her children to complete Sanomi's escape (the youngest girl eventually became a teacher). At the funeral, it appeared that everyone whom had ever come to Winston's Lounge brought plenty of flowers. The patrons also petitioned the University to award Sanomi a posthumous degree.